A Mother's Lament

A Mother's Lament

Lee Gander

RESOURCE *Publications* · Eugene, Oregon

A MOTHER'S LAMENT

Resource Publications
An Imprint of Wipf and Stock Publishers
199 W. 8th Ave., Suite 3
Eugene, OR 97401

www.wipfandstock.com

PAPERBACK ISBN: 978-1-6667-0301-6
HARDCOVER ISBN: 978-1-6667-0302-3
EBOOK ISBN: 978-1-6667-0303-0

06/03/21

This book is dedicated to the millions of babies who will never see the beauty of God's creation, or experience the tender gentle touch of a mother's love.

Contents

Author's Note

A SONG I WROTE many years ago by the same title inspired me to write this book. My passion for the unborn, and the biblical and moral significance of how this understanding affects every aspect of our lives, has driven me to fight for this worthy cause.

For me, the Soul is the essence of our life and identity; recognized by God, at the moment of our conception. How could it be otherwise? The unborn child has a unique personality, heartbeat, fingerprints, etc. By every known identifier that establishes a person's unique and individual identity, an unborn child has it.

What is the human Soul, and why is it valuable? Some place very little importance on the Soul, while others, an immense importance on this unseen part of our human consciousness.

These questions, and their ultimate answers, are what led me to start 'Eternal Soul Ministries'.

God died for, and loves us individually, not corporately. Since our Soul is our identity, the following scriptures give us an insight as to when God begins to recognize our identity: Jeremiah 1:5, and Psalms 139.

Only when we realize the high cost paid for our unique and individual Souls, will we start to respect, cherish, love and value them as God does; *'for God, so loved the world, that He sent His only begotten Son'* to save each and every one, and redeem them back into full holy fellowship with Him.

This familiar scripture, John 3:16, can be personalized to make this point more clear . . .

"For God so loved *you so much*, that He gave His only be-gotten Son, so if *you* believe in Him, *you* will not parish, but have eternal life."

Jesus Christ did not allow Himself to be crucified on Calvary for a cause, but for you personally, your soul and mine. Once we realize this fact fully, we will never doubt our immense personal importance and worth. Paul says confidently, in Romans 8:38, *For I am persuaded, that neither death, nor life, nor angels, nor principalities, nor powers, nor things present, nor things to come, nor height, nor depth, nor any other creature, shall be able to separate us* (you and me) *from the love of God, which is in Christ Jesus our Lord.*

So, you can see why if someone spends an entire lifetime to save just one of these precious Souls, it would be a life well spent, for each human Soul is eternally priceless and infinite in value.

For this reason and more, I present this story of love, loss and redemption.

Lee Gander

PROLOGUE

The Soul

"THE HEART BEATS, THE lungs breathe, the body hungers and thirsts, the flesh seeks pleasure and reels from pain—emotion endlessly fluctuates from the depths of despair and sorrow to the heights of joy and exhilaration; but I, the soul, lost in this chaos of distractions, continue to softly but relentlessly whisper, "Heart, you will cease to beat; Lungs, your breath will stop; Body, you will turn to dust; Passion, you will fade away, but I, your soul, will live on and on and on for eternity."

"Mind, I patiently long to get your attention before time brings your thinking to an end, yet seldom do you give me a thought! I continue to tug against the ever-present throng of worldly cares and pleasures and ask, 'what will you do about me? Are you even aware that I'm here? Do you realize that I am the eternal part of your being?'

Long after everything else has been consumed and gone, I will be. The body spends all its energy on the momentary needs and desires of this temporary life—in vanity it exercises, builds and plans— but what value does it place on me? When will the wasting away give priority to the eternal?

"I pray that my existence will be realized and proper redemptive action taken, before it is too late!"

"How beautiful he is," Mary said to her husband as she picked up her newborn from his bed. Her face radiated awe, as she pondered the many mysteries surrounding her infant child. Mary reflected on the events leading up to this amazing birth—the fear, the scorn, the gossip—but she didn't allow her mind to ponder these dreadful things for even a moment, for she knew who her baby was and had at least a veiled idea of his importance to the world.

She looked into his eyes and remembered all the strange but wonderful events that had occurred in the last year. An angel from God proclaiming this supernatural conception, resulting in the child she now held in her arms; her aunt, well beyond child-bearing years, miraculously becoming pregnant with her son John just a few months earlier. It reminded her of Abraham's wife Sarah and the birth of Isaac according to the ancient Mosaic scrolls. She pondered the host of angels that filled the sky proclaiming her child's birth to the shepherds on the adjacent hill, and the strange circumstances that led the Son of God to be born in a stable with only an animal-feeding trough filled with hay available for his bed. The depth of Mary's love for this Holy Child from God overwhelmed her, as he could not be compared to any other. She knew no mortal would ever again give birth to the one and only Messiah, Jesus Christ, the Savior of the world.

Now, as wonderfully important as this story is, the following is not about Mary and her miraculous Child however, but another mother and child. Told not in the rugged hills of some far-off distant, desolate land centuries ago, but a story that is taking place today, in the comfort of our twenty-first century world, where beds are not filled with straw, and childbirth no longer occurs in caves or barns among the animals. This story is about Gloria and her daughter, just an average mother and child from an average middle-class family in an average American neighborhood. Yet these two precious souls will learn together their immeasurable value and the true depth of their love, as their lives unfold together.

"For you formed my inward parts; you wove me in my mother's womb. I will give thanks to You for I am fearfully and wonderfully made; wonderful are Your works, and my soul knows it very well. My frame was not hidden from You when I was made in secret, and

skillfully wrought in the depths of the earth; Your eyes have seen my unformed substance; and in your book were written the days that were ordained for me, when yet there were not one of them. How precious also are Your thoughts to me, O God! How vast is the sum of them!" (Psalm 139:13–17)

1

A Child is Born

"I BEG OF YOU, Gloria, don't do this! I love you and always will, but do not do this!" Gloria carefully unfolded a note that she had crumpled moments earlier and read it again, and then placed it back in her pocket. The note was from her husband, Jim. They had been having a heated disagreement lately, but Gloria couldn't think of that now. She was resolute, and in spite of Jim's protests, determined to move forward. She loved Jim with all her heart, but this was her decision, and she was convinced something had to be done. So with a sad heart, and reflecting endearingly on Jim's note, she drifted off into a deep sleep.

Upon awaking, Gloria stared lovingly and longingly into the dark eyes of her beautiful newborn, and though she knew this modern-day child of hers was not miraculously conceived as Mary's baby Jesus had been, Gloria's child was no less a miracle and special in her eyes.

Gloria sat comfortably in her hospital room looking with amazement at her precious newborn daughter, nestled and sleeping securely in her arms. Love emanating from her eyes, and overwhelmed with a depth of passion in her heart, she contemplated their future together. She thought of all the many joys and laments that they would inevitably face, and knew the instant her baby was born; the bond of their love would never waiver.

The morning glow of the sun streamed through window blinds in Gloria's birthing room, creating a mosaic pattern of lines throughout the room. She was so distracted and entranced in her admiration of her baby girl that she barely noticed the clamor of footsteps and voices in the hallway through the slightly opened door.

"Gloria?" a soft voice, almost a whisper, filtered into the room as the door slowly opened with a moaning sound.

"We're here!" another subdued voice murmured quietly, stirring Gloria from her surreal trance-like state.

"Oh, look at that baby—isn't she just the most adorable thing you've ever seen?" A chorus of exclamations and admirations echoed as two women invaded Gloria's once-peaceful sanctum.

Knowing immediately to whom the two voices belonged, Gloria looked up to see her two best friends enter the room, ooing and aahing, and making no little fuss over the infant in Gloria's arms. There was a harmonious symphony of wonder, congratulations and excitement for several minutes, before the threesome settled down for a wonderful hour as they shared their mutual admiration of this new life.

"I hope you don't mind us barging in like this, Gloria, but we just had to see your little baby for ourselves before you went home from the hospital," one of Gloria's friends said as the other wholeheartedly agreed.

"Not at all," Gloria said with an approving smile as the baby herself, seemingly in unison with her mother, produced what appeared to be an equally charming smile. "It is so wonderful to have you both here."

Frances, the most conservatively dressed of the two, and known as the "fanatical Christian" in this circle of friends, had married her high school sweetheart, Tom, and was Gloria's next-door neighbor. She noticed right away the small hospital wristband just above the infant's little hand with the baby's name on it.

"Well, that's an odd way of spelling 'Jeni,'" Frances blurted out. "Don't get me wrong, God bless it, it's a lovely name, but why the odd spelling?"

Commiserating with the comment instead of being offended by it, Gloria graciously, and with respect to her husband Jim, explained their disagreement over the spelling and her eventual acceptance of Jim's insistence for it. Gloria had written in the correct spelling of Jeni's name with a marker, as the hospital had mistakenly entered into their computer records a more common spelling of that name.

"It was Jim's idea to spell it in an unconventional way; you know how he is," Gloria confided, somewhat apologetically.

"Jim does have a unique and artistic personality," Frances added.

"He really enjoys putting his creative mind to just about everything," Gloria's other friend, Elle, volunteered. Elle, a widow now for a little over a year, met Gloria while working at a local attorney's office. She had short blonde hair and was the earthiest of her friends. When at work, She dressed conservatively enough in suits or dresses; however, today was a 'casual' day. On these days she typically wore apparel that needed more material in the most essential places.

The two saw a flush of red appear on Gloria's cheeks, as a veiled ire flashed across her face.

"I'm clearly not as adventurous as Jim," Gloria responded defensively.

"And clearly not as stubborn," Elle quipped sarcastically.

"I did protest, but to no avail," Gloria answered with a sigh and a resolved shrug of the shoulders. "The mutilated name will have to stand. There is, however, an interesting story behind the name." Gloria continued, as her face softened with the thought. "Have you heard of a missionary by the name of Gladys Aylward, Frances?" She asked, looking up at Frances, assuming every Christian would know about missionaries, as Frances acknowledged with a nod.

Gloria went on to explain that the spelling of Jeni's name was inspired by Gladys Aylward, a missionary to inland China during the middle of the twentieth century. Miss Aylward was a devoted and determined missionary, on whose life the movie entitled *Inn of the Sixth Happiness* was made. Because of her Christian love and devotion, Miss Aylward was affectionately nicknamed 'Jeni', which means 'Person who loves', by all that knew her.

"Well," Elle volunteered, attempting to divert the conversation from religion, a subject she dreaded, back to the uniquely spelled name, "leave it to Jim anyway, to put his artistic fingerprint on everything he touches; even his child's name,"

"Oh, I like it." Gloria finally relented with acquiescence. "I'm going to love her like crazy, no matter what her name is, or how it is spelled."

"Here, here!" Frances exclaimed, cheerfully agreeing with Gloria's new-found resolution.

Soon the trio returned again to the main event cooing peacefully in Gloria's arms, as they passed the cherished little dark-eyed, dark-haired, healthy baby around from one to another.

"You know, Elle, if you would just add an inch or so of fabric to that dress, you wouldn't be so self-conscious and distracted by it all the time," Frances said teasingly, noticing Elle pulling at first one end of her dress, then the other.

"Well, it's the latest fashion, and you will just have to deal with it," Elle, answered defiantly, a little offended. "I wear the most stylish and trendy clothes, no matter how uncomfortable."

"And no matter how revealing," Frances retorted with a playful smile.

"Gloria, you must bring little 'Jen' to the office after you get settled in," Elle said, brushing off Frances's predictable little jest. "It will be such a riot to see everyone's astonished faces as they see the queen of independence and freedom, with a little ball and cha. . ., I mean, the cutest little ball and chain there ever was."

Gloria and Elle had worked at the local law office together for years, until she had to give up her position to care for Jim after a serious work accident. Gloria went on to be Jim's fulltime caregiver until his recovery, and though she never did return to the office, she and Elle had remained the best of friends through the years.

"Yes, I remember saying that having children would 'cramp' Jim's and my style', but I don't feel that way anymore." Then looking down dreamily at her little Jeni, now back in her own loving arms, she added, "Just look at her. . . isn't she beautiful?"

"God has blessed you mightily, Gloria." Frances said reflectively, with an air of wonderment, revealing a much deeper, intense feeling of emotion than her admiration alone. "Children are fearfully and wonderfully made and known so intimately by God, even before they are even born, or even conceived!"

"Don't you ever get tired of that God stuff?" Elle jabbed, jolting Frances from her dreamy thoughts, as Elle gently backhanded Frances's arm.

Gloria looked at her two friends admiringly, knowing Elle's comment to Frances was misguided and even rude, but also knowing there was a bond, a respect that transcended any squabble or offense, and that there was a deep sentimental reason for the warmness of their close friendship.

"Never mind," Elle added quickly, trying to ward off the expected criticism she knew would quickly follow, adding, "to each their own."

"Elle," Gloria responded, "sometimes you can be just plain . . ."

"It's okay," Frances quickly intervened, throwing water on the burning embers of what could easily erupt into a blaze. "She didn't mean anything by it. Let's not spoil this special day."

So, with emotions calmed and a looming disaster averted, these three special friends settled into a joyful and pleasant afternoon together, pampering and doting over little Jeni.

2

Homeward Bound

WITH HER FRIENDS DEPARTED and the brilliance of the afternoon sun now beating through the windowpanes, sending the once tranquil air into waves of rhythmic dance, Gloria returned to the surreal quietness of the moment. She inspected every little finger and toe and marveled at Jeni's delicate and wondrous features. In every movement she saw the child's intense craving for life, as Jeni's eyes, now wide open, seemed to take in everything that could be seen around her.

She already has such a unique one-of-a-kind personality, Gloria thought as she fell again into a dreamland of wonder about their future together. There would be the school years, friends, college, wedding, husband, and eventually, wincing a little at the thought, *grandchildren*. As Gloria was deep in her dreams, a light knock at the door once again broke the tranquil silence.

"Gloria, it's time to get ready to go." A voice whispered softly from the doorway. It was Caroline, Jeni's nurse.

"Hello, anyone home?" Another voice echoed a second later, startling the nurse and lacking the same thoughtful quiet reverence. Jim had arrived to chauffer Gloria and Jeni home.

"Shhh," Gloria said, with a finger to her lips. "Jeni is sleeping."

"You will find that's a good thing," the nurse whispered to Jim whimsically as they passed through the doorway.

"I'm almost ready," Gloria said, pushing away her wondrous daydreaming for the time being.

Realizing his earlier gaffe, Jim made a more concerted effort to sit quietly next to Gloria and Jeni on the birthing room's pillowed couch. "How's our little angel today?" He asked in a whisper. The radiant glow from the new mother's face answered without words.

"Isn't she just adorable?" Gloria asked, looking up at Jim. "In my imagination, we've lived our entire lives together in just these few short hours."

Just then, Caroline entered with a moving cart, as Jim got up to start getting ready to go.

Caroline helped load Gloria and Jeni's gifts and personal items onto the cart as Jim assisted Gloria into a wheelchair. Pushing his wife, with little Jeni on her lap, Jim led the small procession toward the exit and to the awaiting car.

Jim took his precious daughter from Gloria, and after holding her dreamily for a few moments, gently secured her into her tiny car seat, and then helped Gloria into the passenger seat. Going home would be the first major adventure of Jeni's short life.

After thanking the hospital staff for their wonderful and generous care, Gloria and Jim took little Jeni and set off for home with grand expectations and unknown adventures awaiting them.

Exhausted by all the commotion of being fussed over, and now, due to the rhythmic motion of the melodic sway and humming tones of the car, Jeni fell into a deep, restful sleep. She was oblivious to the streets, signs, buildings, turns and maneuvers needed to get from the hospital to home, and was content to just enjoy, for now, the only small little world she knew at this point of her short life.

The late afternoon sun was now shimmering and pulsating through the budding trees and between the various buildings and structures as they drove up one street and then down another. There was a cool spring chill in the air, as well as the melting snow revealing the winter's accumulation of dead grass, mud and debris. Yet, distracted only by the excitement and thoughts of their precious passenger sleeping soundly behind them, Gloria and Jim were oblivious to these mundane common observances. Their minds were full of the anticipation and excitement of returning home to their familiar and comfortable surroundings, with one very important addition.

"Look there!" Gloria said quietly, but with an intense irritation in her voice, pointing at the Crest Point Cemetery, as if noticing it for the first time.

"It looks like a 'City of Stones' to me," Jim observed casually.

"They shouldn't put those right out in the open where people can see them," she said, maintaining her incredulous tone. "They are frightful places that should be hidden from view!"

"What made you think of that?" Jim responded in a whisper. "It's just the nature of things," he added, in a cold, matter-of-fact way.

"I know," Gloria said, calming a little as the cemetery was now out of sight, "I just can't imagine our little Jeni ending up in a place like that."

"Well, I'm sure it will be quite a while before we need to think about things like that," Jim mused with a little more compassion.

"You know, Jim, Elle's husband, the senator, is buried there."

Just then, a faint cry distracted them from their melancholy thoughts, reminding them of the vibrant life evident behind them. Jeni's presence would often bring a profound joy to their lives in the years to come, but for now, the fussing and crying coming from the back seat, and becoming more intense with each mile, needed their immediate attention.

Painted by the setting sun, a canopy of beautiful and brilliantly colored wisps of billowing clouds illuminated Jeni's homecoming.

"Well, the house doesn't look as bad as I expected," Gloria said playfully, as Jim came through the door loaded down with luggage and other odds and ends. Jim responded with side glance and a good-natured sarcastic smile, for her un-amusing comment.

It wasn't long before Jeni was again fast asleep in her new crib, for a short time anyway. Thoroughly exhausted, Jim and Gloria could finally put their feet up for an hour or two, aware that little Jeni would need attention again, all too soon.

When the morning sun dawned the next day, obeying God's dutiful command to return again to the eastern sky, Jeni found herself lovingly nestled in her mother's arms being slowly rocked back and forth to a soft soothing melody Gloria was humming.

As Jeni was finding satisfaction and nourishment, Gloria looked admiringly at Jeni's newly furnished room. It was meticulously decorated with alphabet blocks, dolls, lace curtains and other trinkets and gifts of all kinds. Some items were store-bought, some beautifully handcrafted by loving hands, and some custom made by Jim in his unique style. Jeni stirred a little in Gloria's arms as the morning sun began to illumine the room.

Jeni was covered with a beautifully embroidered blanket made by Frances and Elle's own skillful hands, one of the most elegant creations in the room. Even Jim had to reluctantly admit that it was a very impressive work of art, even given his own high artistic standards.

A baby book was prominently displayed on the dresser, along with baby shoes, and a cross necklace that hung lazily over a picture frame. A little ones-y lay to one side and other brilliantly colored items were carefully arranged for their best effect; not that Jeni herself would ever appreciate, or notice such loving care.

There was one thing however, to Gloria's irritation, notably missing among Jeni's many beautiful ornaments. There was no *store-bought* item at all with Jeni's name on it. *I don't blame them*, Gloria mused sarcastically to herself. *After all, there isn't any profit in trying to sell items with that spelling.*

"Jim, I forgot to tell you," Gloria exclaimed, at breakfast later that morning, "the strangest thing happened yesterday just before you came to bring baby and me home from the hospital. An oddly dressed man I've never seen before, though he seemed somewhat familiar, came to visit me, or, I should say, visit Jeni. Because I assumed he was an associate of yours, I didn't think too much about it. He treated Jeni and me so kindly, as though we were life-long friends."

"Mmmm . . . "Jim responded with a concerned skepticism. "Did you get his name?"

"No," Gloria responded regretfully, "I didn't think to ask him at the time. As I think back on him now though, I would say he was quite peculiar in his manner."

"Did you feel threatened at all?" Jim asked, now a little concerned over the revelation.

"No, on the contrary, there was such a gentleness about him that when I looked into his eyes, I felt a wonderful peace come over me."

"What did he want? What did he look like?" Jim asked with a deepening concern.

"You're not jealous, are you?" Gloria teased. Jim was not amused, and with a look he encouraged Gloria to move the conversation along.

"Well, he looked like he was in his thirties, wore kind-of-a loose fitting frontiersman-type outfit made with a fabric of large beaded thread, a wide leather belt, sandals, and had long hair with a well-groomed beard and mustache. "

"Sandals at this time of year?"

"Yeah, that's what I thought."

"Well, I don't know anyone who looks remotely like that," Jim said with an incredulous laugh. "At least not since my wild college days." He wondered if Gloria was actually pulling his leg with that description. However, seeing the earnestness in her eyes, he probed again for more information. "So, what did he want?"

"I'm not really sure," Gloria said, pausing reflectively, " . . . to see Jeni I guess." Gloria was now somewhat perplexed herself, as she started to replay the odd encounter with this stranger in her mind. "He said some kind of blessing over her, saying my little girl was very special and that we would see him again someday."

"How strange . . ."

3

Skeeta, Skoota and the Stranger

THE NEXT FEW YEARS of Jeni's young carefree life seemed to fly by un-eventfully, until one evening Gloria approached Jim with a troubling observation. Having emerged from the 'terrible twos' unscathed, Jeni was full of life and had quite a vivid imagination. Her four-year-old imagination, however, was becoming a little too creative for Gloria's taste. So, after being smothered with hugs and kisses, as was their nightly routine, and Jeni safely tucked away and sleeping for the night, Gloria took this opportunity to discuss her concern for Jeni's overall health and emotional well-being with her husband.

"Jim, do you think it's normal for a four-year old to have such a vivid imagination?"

"What do you mean?" Jim responded, lowering his book to give Gloria his full attention.

"You know, Skeeta and Skoota, Jeni's little friends."

Gloria was hoping for a thoughtful response, but only received a careless chuckle from Jim with an apathetic, "Oh, that."

"Jim, I'm serious!" Gloria scolded, this time demanding Jim's full attention. "The other day I went to sit next to Jeni at the kitchen table, when she let out a blood-curdling scream and with flailing arms yelled, 'Stop! You can't sit there!' Evidently, Skeeta, or Skoota, I'm not exactly sure which one, was eating breakfast with her and I was about to sit on one of them! I was then informed that I couldn't sit next to her until her little friends were finished eating and off to play!"

Lost for a moment in the humor of the thought, Jim was about to respond when Gloria interrupted.

"Seriously, the other day when I was vacuuming the living room she asked if I could turn the vacuum cleaner off, because Skeeta and Skoota were watching T.V. in the den and couldn't hear the show. Jeni wasn't even in the same room; she was in the kitchen having a snack!"

Jim wasn't exactly sure how to respond, not having a strong opinion one way or the other. Still, Gloria was pressing him for an immediate response, leaving the safe choice of silence out of the question. Jim quickly formulated two possible approaches on the subject. One option was to dissuade and relieve Gloria by trying to minimize her concerns, and the other was to empathetically commiserate with her. The first, however, could unwittingly backfire and convey an apathetic attitude toward those concerns, while the other might increase Gloria's fears and come across as being disingenuous. Jim concluded that both options were flawed, but Gloria had him in a corner, and there was nowhere to run.

"Now, Gloria, I wouldn't be too concerned about it," Jim said, venturing into the unknown. "It's probably just a normal childhood phase that children go through. I've heard of many children at that age with vivid imaginations."

As soon as his thoughtless reference to 'many children' left his mouth, he knew he had made a fatal blunder, and if challenged, had no official source to back up his claim. To Jim's great relief, however, Gloria didn't notice, or chose not to challenge his faux pas, and instead focused solely on her immediate concern for Jeni.

"Do you think we should call a doctor or something to see if her behavior is normal?" Gloria asked a little less excitedly now, seeing in Jim's eyes at least a nominal concern. "Have you seen anything to be concerned about?" She asked, wondering if Jim had experienced similar behaviors.

"Well, there is one." Jim said, clearing his throat as he reflected for a moment. "The other day while driving to the store, Jeni was unusually quiet. I thought she might have fallen asleep, so I quietly asked if she was indeed sleeping. 'No, Daddy,' she responded. 'I'm just sitting here contemplating the end of the world.' Can you imagine such a statement, and she said it so matter-of-factly."

After relating this story to Gloria, Jim, now found himself empathizing a little more with Gloria's concerns. "I wasn't only shocked by the apocalyptic nature of her statement," Jim continued, "but, 'contemplating'? How does a four-year-old even understand the meaning of a word like that?"

"You're kidding!" Gloria exclaimed, as she remembered a recent discussion that had occurred at her 'Book Club' meeting with the girls.

"I asked why she would be 'contemplating' such a horrific thing as the end of the world and she told me that on one of your 'talk nights', you were talking about one hundred pound hail or something like that, that would fall from the sky when the world comes to an end, and that a lot of people would hate God because of it."

"She was listening?" Gloria cringed, horrified at the thought! "Oh, that Frances and that evil book!" she said with indignation and disgust. "How Frances can revolve her life around such a medieval, outdated book of violence, superstitions and myths, I'll never know!" And then added, "I know Elle feels the same way!"

"I can certainly agree with you on that," Jim concurred, clearly commiserating with Gloria's sentiments on that issue.

"Frances will not be sharing anymore of that book with us from now on, I'll guarantee you that!" Gloria finished with emphasis.

That night's conversation ended without a clear plan of action but an agreement that more information about Jeni's peculiar behavior was needed. Soon however, their concern for Jeni's vivid imagination would only become more troubling; for while Gloria and Jim were having their conversation in the living room, another conversation was taking place in Jeni's room.

Hi, Captain." Jeni greeted a stranger standing next to her bed as she put a finger to her lips, urging him to be very quiet. "Skeeta and Skoota are sleeping."

"Are you feeling afraid?" The stranger asked softly. "Has the darkness frightened you?"

"I'm having that claustr-r-o-ph-pho-bia-ic feeling again," Jeni admitted, not quite knowing exactly how to pronounce the word, but understanding its meaning.

"Yes, I know," The stranger said with a warm reassuring whisper, while gently caressing Jeni's soft dark curls. "That's why I'm here."

Jeni didn't often have these feelings of fear and isolation, but whenever she did, the stranger, who Jeni now knew as the Captain, would appear, to comfort and reassure her that everything was all right and that there was nothing to be afraid of.

Soon Jeni closed her eyes and was sleeping peacefully again, as the stranger also vanished from the room and her thoughts.

4

Elle's Loss—Paul's Gain: Part 1

ELLE'S HUSBAND PAUL HAD died just over a year before Jeni was born, and around the same time Frances had had a devastating still-birth that almost destroyed her life and marriage. And, although Paul and Jeni were never to meet this side of heaven, he nonetheless would still become an integral part of her life story.

Once a strong and commanding personality as well as a highly respected state senator, Paul found himself in a battle unrelated to politics as he suffered the indignities of disease and spiritual confusion. Elle's grief was inconsolable, but made easier by the love and support of her two best friends.

Elle and Paul met in college while studying law, married, and soon after enjoyed successful careers. Paul went into politics and was elected senator a few years later, while Elle joined a prestigious law firm in the neighboring district. Their careers consumed their lives, so they had little time to start or raise a family. They both talked about having children and how they desired them, and once, Elle even found she was pregnant. However, with that pregnancy coming at the time their careers were just beginning to blossom, that 'inconvenience' was quickly taken care of. So, as the years slipped steadily by, they enjoyed what most would consider to be a good life.

Hey, guys, it is so good to see you again!" Paul said, greeting Frances and her husband Tom, as they entered his hospital room. "Just put your coats anywhere," he said invitingly.

Now about one year into his treatments, Paul had been admitted to the hospital to receive an infusion of antibiotics due to a bout of pneumonia caused by his compromised immune system. Paul had asked Frances and Tom to visit him, due to the progression and escalation of his illness .

"Come in and sit down. How's the baby?" he asked, looking at Frances struggle a little to sit down and get comfortable. "It won't be long now, will it?"

"I hope not," Frances said with a sigh, but with a mother's love twinkling in her eyes.

With two sons already in college, this very unexpected, and very unplanned pregnancy, was made even more improbable by the fact that Frances was at the end of her childbearing years. However, after that initial shock was over, their excitement grew daily in anticipation of this new and beautiful life; that was to never be.

"Elle's off taking care of some important business, so this is a good time for us to talk about something that's been on my mind for a while." He said, as the smile that initially welcomed his guests slowly melted into an expression of sober reflection.

"What is it, Paul?" Frances and Tom asked in chorus, seeing the change in his facial expression.

Paul began to reflect upon his life as the rhythmic beeps of the machines and the hustle and bustle in the hallway slowly faded into silence. It was almost Christmas, and Paul wanted to keep the day's news, which was not good to say the least, from Elle through the holidays so as to not put a cloud of sadness over this festive time. But he also wanted to ask Frances and Tom a favor that he stressed was most urgent, due to his declining condition.

"When life is full of routines and responsibilities," he began, "the stark realization of a condition like this forces a person to slow down and think beyond the business and distractions of this life. One starts to wonder if there is more to it all." As he continued, a sheepish shyness enveloped his face, almost a look of shame. "Elle and I have never had any use for religion, God or anything like that, but, as I've been listening closely to some of the Christmas carols playing and their message, well. . ." he paused for a moment as an inevitable hopelessness loomed over him. Now with a grave seriousness in his voice, and in lawyer-type fashion, he continued again. "Due to my condition and the fact that I will soon know beyond a shadow of a doubt what lies beyond, I thought it would be rather prudent of me to find out beforehand exactly what, if anything, is on the 'other side' and to discover for myself the truth of the matter."

Frances and Tom were quite shaken and taken off guard by both the hopeless news of Paul's failing health, as well as his bold new interest in the spiritual. On many occasions and with much pride and conviction, Elle and Paul had boasted of their freedom from what they called archaic and juvenile beliefs, and proudly proclaimed their atheism.

Not knowing exactly what to say, for they had never been in this situation before, they felt quite inadequate, but when they started to express their doubts, Paul interrupted.

"Elle says you go to church and has also said on more than one occasion that you are quite fanatical in your beliefs. Is that true?"

"Well, ah . . ." Frances and Tom both began to stumble over their next few words, knowing 'fanatical' was far from how they would characterize their belief system.

Although both Frances and Tom would eventually earn that infamous reputation, it wasn't until after Paul's death and the stillbirth of her child, that they would go on to discover that deeper and more intimate relationship with Jesus.

"W, well . . . we do try to go to church every week and to a Bible study every once in a while," Tom volunteered embarrassingly.

"But I don't know how much help we would be to you," Frances reluctantly chimed in, and then, referring to Paul's last statement with some humiliation, "I don't think we are as fanatical as Elle makes us out to be, but we could ask our pastor to visit if you like."

"I would appreciate that, if you wouldn't mind," Paul said appreciatively, though a little bewildered at their hesitation.

Just then, Elle returned, much to Frances and Tom's relief, and the conversation quickly changed from religion and fanaticism to subjects of more general interest. The four friends spent the next couple of hours enjoying each other's company as they reminisced about days gone by and the many successes and accomplishments Paul had had through the years. Paul, however, was having a very different conversation within his own mind. He wasn't looking back, but forward, toward his unknown and fearful future.

A few weeks later Frances and Tom's pastor, Pastor Dennis, rang the doorbell as the hospice nurse let him in. "Hi Paul," he greeted, entering Paul's makeshift sleeping quarters near the window of his living room. All parties had agreed that placing Paul in the living room instead of the bedroom would make his care both more convenient and comfortable. Pastor Dennis had been a frequent visitor since Paul's release from the hospital a few weeks earlier.

"How are you feeling today, Paul?" Pastor Dennis asked cordially and sympathetically as he sat down next to Paul's bed.

Well, Pastor Dennis," he answered humorously, but with a hint of sarcasm, "Do you see all these machines, bags and tubes? They make me feel fairly tolerable," and then added playfully pointing to one of the machines next to his bed. "Sometimes too good if I turn that knob up too high or leave it on for too long!" Pastor Dennis responded with an enlightened chuckle. "But on a more serious note, Pastor," Paul continued, "When we talked last time I was asking you how a truly loving God could not allow everyone into his heaven and why Jesus is the only way to get there. How could a loving God reject anyone?"

"Actually, Paul, those two questions are closely related," Pastor Dennis said, adjusting Paul's pillow to make him more comfortable. "Let me ask you a question. What do you think of this world and this life?" Now, before Paul's illness, his personal life wasn't so bad; however, he did have to admit that the world as a whole, with all its evils, poverty, crime, sickness and death, was overall a dismal place. With that admission, Pastor Dennis followed up with another question. "Are people generally bad or good?

Paul thought for a few seconds and then answered, "Generally, well. . . some are, and some are not."

"Then, if those 'bad' people were all allowed to go to heaven in the name of God's love, wouldn't heaven just become another corrupt 'bad' place?"

"I've never thought of it quite like that," Paul responded reflectively. "Your logic is sound."

Pastor Dennis kept to the theme of 'Is God Good?'. "In our last meeting you said you could no longer identify as an atheist, because you now see the logical and complex design of this universe having evolved through random chance as an absolute impossibility; and I agree with you whole-heartedly. However, if we conclude that there must be a grand designer, a first cause so-to-speak, or a god if you will, then you must ask yourself: why would an all-powerful being create a universe corrupted by evil? "

Paul listened quietly until Pastor Dennis raised his Bible high, and looking him squarely in the eyes said passionately, "Paul, if your god is not the God of this Bible or the Father of Jesus Christ, then I would vehemently hate your god, and would rather go to your god's hell than to serve him!" Wincing at such strong emotion coming from his new clergy friend, Paul involuntarily drew back a little.

"I shocked you, didn't I, Paul?" Pastor Dennis said playfully as he relaxed back into his chair with a smile. "I didn't mean to startle you, but I did want to drive home the point and get your attention. I'll explain . . . "

Paul, after recovering from Pastor Dennis's premeditated passionate rant, held out his hand to indicate that not only was he not offended, but that he also appreciated Pastor Dennis's passion for both his friendship and concern for his soul.

Pastor Dennis took Paul's hand of friendship while placing his other on Paul's shoulder.

"Paul, if some god created this fishbowl we call Earth merely to watch us suffer and die in its meaningless existence, then in my opinion, that god would be pure evil!" Dennis did not mince his words, and it was clear that he had pondered this question long and hard for some time. "We may never fully understand why there is pain and suffering, but there is one thing we know beyond a shadow of a doubt, and that is the God of this Bible, my God, came here to suffer with us, sending His only begotten Son, Jesus Christ, to experience our same pain, suffering and death."

Tears came to Paul's eyes as he realized for the first time all he had missed in his life and that it had taken a serious illness to show him what true life was all about. Pastor Dennis never knew why those tears came, and assumed it was due to the pain Paul so often suffered on his visits, but Paul knew. At that very moment, Paul had felt the loving touch of his Savior's love, and had experienced first-hand, the eternal life-changing miracle of God's amazing grace in his soul.

As Pastor Dennis finished making his point, Paul couldn't help but chuckle a little inside, as he realized that his own suffering and imminent death had led him to his cross of salvation.

"Well, it's getting late, Paul," Pastor Dennis said with a yawn, "so let's leave the 'Why only Jesus?' question for Friday's meeting. In the meantime, here is a little booklet called *Living On the Sun* that might help you gain some insight on the subject of why even 'good' people can't go to heaven without Jesus."

Dennis prayed with Paul before leaving, and Paul thanked him for his friendship and for being so generous with his time.

Later that night when all was quiet, Paul opened up the little booklet . . .

5

Elle's Loss—Paul's Gain: Part 2

(Excerpts from "Living on the Sun")

Living on the Sun

CAN YOU OR *I live on the sun? Did you know that sinners like you and me could no more live on the sun than live in the presence of a holy and perfect God?*

This is what God said to Moses on Mount Sinai. "You cannot see my face, for no man can see Me and live." If we, as sinners, cannot see God and live, how can we be with Him in heaven and live?

Now, getting back to the sun, if you or I could be 'transformed' into fire, we would no longer be in danger of the sun's destructive forces and could easily go there and freely roam around on its surface and enjoy all the wonders and amazing things to discover there. We could actually live on the sun!

In the same way, if a sinful soul could be 'transformed' into holiness, into the likeness and character of God, we could freely go be with Him, enjoy His heaven and all the infinite wonders and amazing things we could discover there, in His presence!

Paul lowered the book to reflect on what he had just read. The analogy did not escape his intellect or logic, but it was also clear that it would be just as impossible for a person to be transformed into fire as it would to be transformed into holiness. He read on . . .

God has little interest in our ability to live on the sun. However, He has a great interest in our ability to be with Him; a desire so great in fact, that He sent His only begotten Son, Jesus Christ, to suffer and die on a cruel Roman cross to make that possible! Consider the following verses. . .

"For God so loved the world that He gave His only begotten Son, that whosoever believes in Him, will not perish, but have everlasting life." John 3:16

"But because of His great love for us, God, who is rich in mercy, made us alive with Christ even when we were dead in our sins—it is by grace you have been saved. And God raised us up (transformed us) in Christ and seated us with Him in the heavenly realms in Christ Jesus." Ephesians 2:4–6

". . . who, by the power that enables Him (Jesus Christ) to bring everything under His control, will 'transform' our lowly (sinful) bodies so that they will be like His glorious (holy) body." Philippians 3:21

These verses clearly show us the transforming power that can and will change us from 'sin' (un-holiness) to 'Glory' (holiness) through the blood of Jesus Christ, and why so many Christians find comfort when facing death. They don't just fantasize or imagine there is a better life beyond the grave; they know it!

"O death, where is your sting? O grave, where is your victory? 1 Corinthians 15:55

Christians no longer need to fear death, but actually see it as the blessed gateway to receiving the full and complete victory over it!

What a wonderful truth and clear analogy Paul thought, *and not just some hopeless fantasy or invention of the mind, but a real Truth that is clearly revealed right in the Bible for 'anyone' to discover for themselves!*

When Pastor Dennis came to see Paul the following week, he sadly noticed that Paul's remaining time was short. He also noticed a change in Paul; there was a peace about him that he had not seen before.

Although Paul was so weak and could no longer sit up in bed, his mind was still sharp, and as strength permitted, enjoyed talking passionately about the friends he would soon miss and the 'bucket list' he would never complete. But mostly of Elle, the love of his life.

Paul also knew his time was short, and although salvation and Christianity was no longer a mystery, or a myth to him, he still had some lingering doubts of his being worthy of God's love and forgiveness. The guilt of his past overwhelmed him.

"I've done so many bad things in my life," Paul admitted to Pastor Dennis with tears of regret. "Do I need to confess them to you?"

"No, Paul, that won't be necessary," Pastor Dennis responded with compassion. "God knows your heart and has already washed it clean."

"But I've supported legislation that has cost the lives of thousands, maybe millions! Oh, Dennis!" he cried out, "all those babies! Their innocent blood on my hands!" Paul turned away with all his remaining strength to bury his face in his pillow. Pastor Dennis could only put a sympathetic hand on his shoulder and wait for the storm to pass.

"That is why Jesus shed His blood, Paul, so that you and I would not have to bear the guilt of sins and misguided decisions," Dennis reassured him, breaking the silence. "Jesus took our griefs and bore our sorrows on the cross. You no longer need to feel guilty; He understands. His great love has taken that guilt from you. That is what being transformed is all about; Jesus took our guilt upon himself and replaced it with His Holiness! You may not always feel forgiven, but God's promises are true. God cannot break a promise! Paul, you are clean!"

Though comforted by Pastor Dennis's words, lingering doubts still remained.

"What can I do to make up for my sin? How can I, with no time left, make amends for all I've done wrong?" Paul asked in despair with pleading eyes.

"You don't have to!" Pastor Dennis said passionately, moving his chair a little closer and leaning forward. "Let me tell you a story about a man who was in your exact situation many years ago. We don't know his name, but we know his fate. He was a criminal, a thief, maybe even a murderer. He was found guilty and sentenced to death by crucifixion with two other men, a criminal like himself, and the other, our blessed Savior. At first this criminal joined the chorus of mockers in the crowd, taunting Jesus, saying that if He was truly the Christ, the Son of God, He could save Himself and them from their suffering and inevitable death."

Paul listened intently as Dennis further explained that this criminal hanging next to Jesus, who was at first belligerent, had a change of heart and started to believe that Jesus was truly the Son of God, eventually defending Jesus and rebuking the others for their cruel and misguided accusations.

"Paul," Pastor Dennis said with conviction, "this criminal was nailed to a cross. There was no way he could make any restitution. He wasn't even able to return whatever he had stolen. He wasn't able to perform one good deed to make up for his life of sin and rebellion! So, he did the only thing he could do, or you and I can do for that matter: he looked to Jesus for mercy and forgiveness, and this is what Jesus said to him, '*Truly I say to you, today you will be with me in paradise.*'

"So, that's all? Just freely ask?" Paul responded with astonishment.

"Yes, Paul," Dennis answered. "It's that simple. It's that free. Believe on the Lord Jesus Christ and you will be saved."

The following week would be their last meeting, as Paul was very weak now, and would soon succumb to the inevitable.

"Since . . . th . . . this most likely will be our la . . . last meeting," Paul said, breathing heavily with great effort, struggling to speak, "I . . . I would like you to do me a fa . . . favor."

"Sure, Paul, what is it?"

"Th . . . the drawer," Paul said, struggling to point at a night-stand next to his bed. "I want you t . . . to give that to Elle w . . . when I'm gone."

Pastor Dennis opened the drawer and pulled out a Bible, another book and an envelope with Elle's name on it.

"In . . . in one year . . . " Paul concluded with difficulty.

Pastor Dennis, understanding the request, assured Paul he would do as he wished.

"I no longer fear d . . . death, but will miss . . . you . . . an . . . and Elle. " Paul struggled to say as Pastor Dennis stood to leave for what would be their last farewell.

"Goodbye, my friend," Pastor Dennis said, with tear-filled eyes.

A few days later Paul passed away peacefully at home, surrounded by his family. When Pastor Dennis heard of Paul's passing, he knelt down, and remembered again Jesus' words to the thief on the cross, *Truly I say to you, 'today' you will be with me in paradise.*

So Paul was laid to rest in that City of Stones; Pastor Dennis, reminding them all in his tribute, that stark and vivid truth from Scripture . . . *for it is appointed unto man once to die and after that the judgment.*

Elle had lost her husband, but Paul had gained heaven and an eternity with Jesus; where there will be *'no more death, no more loneliness, no more pain and no more tears.'*

6

Jeni's First Day of School

"YOUR FIRST DAY OF school," Gloria said with a heavy sigh. She had been dealing all week with numerous emotions ranging from joy to fear to grief.

"Oh, Mommy, you're not going to get all mushy on me again, are you?" Jeni replied with a polite, but whimsical sarcasm.

"No need of that, sweet-heart," Gloria assured Jeni with a hug and a kiss. "At least not until you've gone."

"Oh, Mommy," Jeni groaned again with a sigh, "I love you."

Gloria continued to annoy Jeni throughout the morning with a myriad of warnings, cautions and reminders. Even Jim could not temper or dissuade Gloria's fears and excitement of the morning; but as expected and as most first days of school go, it started and ended without incident—at least for Jeni.

Later that morning Frances received a frantic phone call. "Gloria, is that you? What's wrong?" Frances asked, sensing the urgency in Gloria's voice. Frances rushed out the front door, grabbing her car keys. "What can I do to help?"

"Right after I sent Jeni off to school this morning that stupid side pain I've been having ever since Jeni's birth started up again— worse than ever, and Jim isn't answering his phone!" Gloria grimaced through the intense pain.

"I'm in my car now, I'll be there in less than a minute," Frances assured her.

Although they were literally next-door neighbors, Frances thought to take the car in the event that Gloria would need to be rushed directly to the emergency room, which turned out to be the case. Gloria's pain had started soon after Jeni's birth, and at first the pain was just an annoyance, but over time it had intensified and become more frequent.

"It has never been this bad before," Gloria lamented to Frances on the way to the hospital as she held back the natural but embarrassing urge to cry out, wincing instead with subdued groans.

Jim arrived just as the doctor was examining Gloria. Dr. Michaels was an older gentleman with wire-rimmed glasses and thinning gray hair, arrayed in traditional hospital attire that was a little snug for his build.

"I see that this is not the first time you've been seen for this," Dr. Michaels said scanning over Gloria's chart. "So far, we've ruled out appendicitis or any digestive issues, so for now, I feel comfortable giving you something to ease the pain."

After conducting several more tests, the doctor said he would contact Gloria when the test results were available. With that, Dr. Michaels said 'goodbye' and exited the room.

When Jeni returned from school that afternoon, Gloria quickly forgot about her distressing day, especially when she saw how excited Jeni was over her first day of school.

Jeni talked for an hour with her parents about the first day's events and of all her new experiences.

"I met a new friend today!" Jeni exclaimed excitedly with a beaming smile, as she shared the biggest and most thrilling news of all. "Her name is Chloe, and I just know we'll be lifelong best forever friends!"

"That's wonderful," Gloria responded with a pleased smile of her own.

"I still miss Skeeta and Scoota though," Jeni added as her face turned sullen with the thought.

"You don't see them anymore?" Her father asked.

"Well, not really," Jeni said sadly. "But, they seemed so real at the time. I guess they weren't though."

Then, just as Gloria was about to console her baby girl over this sad realization, Jeni's face brightened with excitement. "But I still see the Captain once in a while," she went on to say. "He still visits sometimes when I'm sad or lonely, and sometimes, just for the fun of it!"

Gloria and Jim looked at each other in concerned astonishment as Jeni went on to explain again how unique the Captain looked and how kind and gentle he was. Although Gloria and Jim were surprised over this revelation, they were not overly anxious for Jeni's safety. Jeni's room was secure and had been checked thoroughly on many previous occasions for any evidence of this mysterious intruder, but nothing was ever discovered. The only thing they could do for the present was to ponder why he was still in Jeni's imagination, and hope this aberration of hers would soon fade away into that same enchanted world of forgetfulness as Skeeta and Scoota.

Life for the Johnson family soon returned to its uneventful routine, until several days later when Gloria received the call from Doctor Michaels' nurse.

"Hi, Gloria, this is Trish from Mercy. Dr. Michaels would like to schedule an appointment for you to see a specialist."

The nurse went on to explain that it wasn't because of something the doctor had found wrong, but primarily due to the fact that nothing wrong could be detected. In a way Gloria and Jim were relieved with the news, but they shared an apprehension as to the continuing mystery of Gloria's pain.

The appointment was made, and after seeing that specialist, others followed with no clearer evidence of a diagnosis than the first. Gloria and Jim were understandably frustrated and disappointed; however, there was nothing they could do but wait for answers that at least for now, eluded even the skilled specialists.

7

Jeni and the Captain

"Do you still miss Skeeta and Skoota?" The Captain asked Jeni tenderly, during one of his nightly visits.

"Yes," Jeni answered sadly, sitting on the edge of her bed. "I try to imagine them back, but it doesn't work anymore. I guess that's just part of growing up," she added with a shrug. "After all, I am almost seven, now."

"They were a great comfort to you over the years, weren't they?" The Captain added compassionately, inwardly amused at Jeni's proud accomplishment of attaining almost seven years of life.

"They sure were Cap, but at least you're still here."

"I will always be with you my sweet Jeni, forever and ever," the Captain answered confidently.

"Because you're not in my imagination?" Jeni asked, apprehensively.

"Yes," The Captain said reassuringly. "I am not in your imagination. I am more real than anything you know."

Jeni was quite relieved to hear the Captain's confident reassurance. Because Skeeta and Skoota had disappeared so suddenly, she was fearful he might vanish at any moment as well.

"I am your life." The Captain said, seeing the lingering doubt and uneasiness on her face. "We are one, and no power on earth or in heaven, will ever separate us."

"I hope so." Jeni said sincerely, as she looked up into the Captain's eyes, and then asked curiously. "What is heaven?"

"Oh, Jeni girl," the Captain answered, with a glow of wonderment in his eyes, "it's a beautiful place, full of light, color and life; where there is no loneliness, no pain and no fear at all."

"That sounds like a nice place, Cap."

"It is," The Captain responded softly, giving Jeni a loving embrace goodbye. "I love you, my sweet little Jeni girl. Sleep now, and don't be afraid."

"I won't," Jeni answered with a big smile, returning the Captain's hug.

As Jeni and the Captain's conversation came to an end, another one, just down the hall, was just getting started.

"Remember back when Jeni told us she no longer saw her imaginary friends, Skeeta and Skoota?" Gloria asked Jim, as they were getting ready for bed.

"Yes, and I remember telling you not to worry, that it was just a childhood phase she was going through, and that she would grow out of it," Jim answered, with a slight intimation of pride.

"Well, I wouldn't be so sure," Gloria responded, catching the obvious, I-told-you-so, inflection in Jim's voice.

"Why do you say that?"

"That stranger," Gloria answered, with grave concern, "he's still with us."

"Oh, him," Jim said indifferently.

"Yes him!" Gloria countered back, a little agitated at Jim's ambivalence. "All these years later and he hasn't gone the way of Jeni's other imaginary friends, and frankly, it still gives me the creeps just to think about it."

"Now Gloria, be patient. We know that stranger is as harmless as Jeni's other invisible friends. We've checked her room countless times and found nothing."

"I know, but still . . . "

"Don't worry, Gloria," Jim interjected at Gloria's hesitation. "Give it time. That stranger will eventually go the way of all her other make-believe aberrations; you'll see."

"I sure hope so," Gloria answered, still not entirely convinced, or sharing her husband's confidence.

The next morning flew by in a rush, as Jeni's parents overslept, waking her up later than usual. As a result Jeni's routine was hurried, and before she knew it, she was bounding down the school bus steps in search of her best friend Chloe.

Because Jeni's parents had conveyed such an obvious agitation at the mention of the Captain, Jeni had turned to Chloe to confide in about his visits.

"Chloe!" Jeni said excitedly, after finding her friend in a crowd of students.

"Hi Jeni" Chloe said excited to see her friend.

"Guess what?" Jeni said, mysteriously, in a hushed whisper.

"What?"

"He visited me again last night."

"Really?" Chloe responded, knowing exactly what her friend was talking about. "What happened?"

"I'm glad I can talk with you about him." Jeni reflected, not meaning to ignore Chloe's question.

"Sure, but what happened?" Chloe insisted, now even more impatiently.

"You know I don't talk about him with my parents anymore, because they kinda freak out when I do."

This time, Jeni intentionally evaded Chloe's question, to tease her.

"Jeni!" Chloe finally said exasperated. "You know I hate it when you do that!"

"I know, that's why it's so fun," Jeni answered, mischievously.

"Are you going to tell me, or. . ."

At this point, Jeni knew she had strained Chloe's patience to the max. "Okay, okay, just relax!" Jeni said, with a gesture to dissuade Chloe's wrath.

"You better!" Chloe scowled.

Jeni quickly recounted her conversation with the Captain, until the last warning bell sounded for school to start. As usual, Chloe was mesmerized by Jeni's encounters with her strange friend, and couldn't wait for lunchtime to hear more.

Jeni also found it hard to concentrate on her teacher that day, as she was lost in her own thoughts of the night before, and the nagging feeling that she may never see the Captain again.

Her fears however, were unfounded; and although the Captain's visits did in fact decrease over the subsequent years, she hardly noticed, as the fascinating, ever-expanding discoveries of 'real' life, continued to overshadow her make-believe world.

8

The Diagnosis

THE YEARS FLEW BY for Gloria and Jim as Jeni grew into a healthy good-natured young lady. They had endured the usual inconveniences such as the terrible twos, potty training, toothless smiles, the occasional predictable scrapes and bruises suffered while mastering the art of riding a bicycle and maneuvering a skateboard. Her dark hair was almost to her waist now and her brilliant smile revealed a straight set of brilliant white teeth. Life was good, and she loved every minute of it. Her spirit glowed with the same impatient zest for life her mother had seen in her eyes as an infant those many years ago. But sadly, unseen forces were at work to destroy the beauty of this vibrant life.

"It's time, Gloria," Jim called from the bedroom as he put the last few items needed for their short trip into a suitcase. Gloria and Jim were on their way to an appointment with yet another specialist several hours away.

Plans were made to have Jeni stay with Frances while they were gone. It was the first time Jeni would spend an extended period of time away from her parents, so she was more than a little nervous and excited.

"Frances should be here any minute to pick you up," Gloria yelled to Jeni from the kitchen, while wrapping up a few last minute items of her own.

"It's nice that Tom was called away on business for a few days so Jeni and Frances can really get to know each other, isn't it?" Jim remarked in passing as he hurried down the hallway. "She doesn't talk about God all the time, does she?"

"No, she's harmless. . ."

"Frances is here!" Jeni announced excitedly, as she ran to get the door.

"Hi Jeni, how's my grown up girl this afternoon?" Frances asked with eager anticipation. "We are going to have such a blessedly wonderful time, you and I!"

"Be a good girl," Gloria whispered to Jeni, stealing a quick hug as Jeni and Frances headed out the door.

Soon they were all on their way, each apprehensive concerning their futures. This was uncharted territory for Jeni and Frances, for although they were neighbors and had been for years, they had never really spent any intimate one-on-one time together. As for Gloria and Jim, this was way too familiar territory, because the answers they so desperately wanted, as well as needed, had continued to elude them.

Gloria and Jim's road trip afforded many hours of conversation, but they could muster only a few superficial words, as their thoughts were entangled in quiet reflection and anticipation of the next day's appointment. *Would they finally discover the cause? Would a definitive diagnosis elude the doctors yet again?* This last thought was their worst fear of all.

Still in doubt of the outcome, Gloria and Jim checked in the next morning and sat anxiously in the waiting room for their appointment.

"Gloria, the doctor can see you now," a nurse called out from an opened door near the reception desk.

The nurse led them down a hallway to an examination room, and after a thorough exam, the doctor invited them to return the next morning for the results. This meant that Jeni would have to stay an extra night with Frances.

In the meantime, Frances and Jeni's apprehensions of how they might get along quickly vanished, as they laughed and giggled, played games, baked and talked late into the night. They marveled at how quickly the hours flew by as Jeni shared stories about her best friend Chloe, school interests, vacations and her many silly adventures with Skeeta and Skoota, while Frances shared some of her childhood stories as well.

"It was the best time ever!" Jeni would later say to her parents after they returned home from their appointment. "Being a Christian isn't as boring as you might think."

As Jeni and Frances were sharing a wonderful time together and Gloria and Jim nervously pondered the next day's results, Elle sat in her bed, pondering over an envelope in her hands.

Elle glanced at the nightstand next to her, where a neglected Bible lay, and then back to the item in her hands. With respectful tenderness and reverence, she caressed the mysterious envelope, turning it one way, and then the other. She examined every stroke of every letter on it written by her beloved's own hand: *To my dearest Elle.* She had always admired Paul's unique and flamboyant writing style and was convinced it was one of the reasons he was so successful when they were together . . . she stopped; *no more tears,* she said to herself, raising her chin defiantly. Yet, this defiant resolve didn't keep a few tears from welling up in her eyes and moistening her long lashes.

She quickly turned her attention back to the letter. This habit of caressing the envelope was not foreign to her in the least; it had become a ritual since coming into her possession years earlier and was still unopened. Once she had asked Frances to open it and read it to her, but for obvious sentimental and privacy reasons, Frances graciously and respectfully refused.

So as she had done on each anniversary of Paul's death and occasionally at other times, Elle drew the envelope from the nightstand drawer and held it in wonderment, as an undercurrent of fond memories flooded her mind. But were they all fond memories?

Elle did not consider herself to be superstitious; however, at times she would ponder over the mysterious unknown contents of Paul's letter as if it were a menacing communication from the grave. This overwhelming fear seemed to overshadow her curiosity, and consciously or unconsciously, seemed to be a good enough reason to leave its secrets buried.

How foolish, she thought to herself whenever she held it, but somehow, in the core of her being, and into the depths of her heart, this rare but habitual practice of fondling Paul's letter had turned into some kind of sacred ritual. She couldn't understand its power or why she couldn't just rip it open and get it over with.

Elle glanced again at the Bible on the nightstand. She had never looked beyond its first pages and really had no interest in ever doing so; she was only interested in what was written just inside the front cover: *To my dearest Elle.* As she picked it up and opened it, she saw again the inscription Paul had written with his unique calligraphy-style script. She softly glided her fingertips over the golden words, written with Paul's special gold ink-filled Senate pen, and then returned it apathetically to the nightstand. *Just a book of myths and fairytales,* she murmured.

Elle had no use for the Bible or any other religious book for that matter. She only kept it near her for sentimental reasons and for the fact that Paul had written his affection toward her in it.

As time went by, Elle built what could only be described as an obsessive shrine around this envelope. She was convinced that the moment it was opened and its secrets revealed, there would be closure, and a once-and-for-all end to the truest love she had ever known. With the best of intentions, all her friends lovingly encouraged her to move on and thought she had, but she didn't want to move on, she didn't want closure; she just wanted Paul, even if only as a memory.

There was another reason for leaving the letter's contents a mystery: fear, the fear of re-living anew that immense grief of Paul's passing; a grief now so guarded and buried in Elle's soul, that even her friends were unaware of its lingering power. *I cannot relive my loss of Paul all over again!* She said to herself as she returned the envelope to its hallowed resting place, *I will not relive it!*

The next day Gloria and Jim sat anxiously across from the specialist. He appeared to be looking over some papers on his desk and had what could only be described as a perplexed look on his face; he was obviously hesitant to initiate a conversation.

"Well Mr. and Mrs. Johnson," he began, breaking the uncomfortable silence and clearing his throat. "The results are, for now, inconclusive." *No answers again,* Gloria and Jim lamented quietly in the depth of their souls. "I still have a few more test results to review . . . " he paused as he shuffled around more papers on his desk. "However it is very unlikely that I will have any better success than the previous specialists that have examined you—at least physically that is."

At that statement, Gloria and Jim reacted simultaneously with wide-eyed amazement and incredulity at the doctor's implication.

"Like I said," the doctor reiterated quickly upon seeing Gloria and Jim's stunned reaction, "we have to wait for more results to be sure of anything. In the meantime, take comfort in the fact that I as well have found nothing obvious to be concerned about."

However, these all too familiar words brought no comfort to Gloria and Jim, as the doctor continued. "For now, try to relax, and we will contact you soon as I have more information." With that, the doctor accompanied them back to the waiting room and wished them a good day.

On their way home, Gloria and Jim were quietly absorbed in their own thoughts as the white noise so often unnoticed by the conscious mind, began to swell into a deafening din. Every dip and bump in the road was an annoying shock, as the wind howled past each window with a thunderous moaning. Nerves were strained to the limit as they traveled laboriously mile after mile in silence, until the strain could no longer be contained.

"Mental?" Gloria murmured intensely under her breath, but audible to Jim. "Mental!" she repeated, with added agitation.

"Well, the doctor didn't, ah, actually say, um . . . " Jim hesitated as he cleared his throat, realizing too late he had started an incoherent thought that had no positive conclusion, and he hoped desperately for a miracle to save him. To Jim's relief, Gloria provided that escape.

"Mental! That doctor thinks I'm crazy!" Gloria blurted out, but this time with an angry passion. "Can you believe it?"

Jim shook his head sympathetically, not knowing how to respond. The doctor was clear in his innuendo of Gloria's condition and both felt hopeless and apprehensive. Still not knowing exactly what to say that would dissuade Gloria's anxious fears, Jim reached over to caress the back of her neck, knowing at times like this, it always helped to calm her nerves.

They again, managed a few words of superficial conversation, but for the most part, they spent the long ride home in uncomfortable silence.

9

The School Incident

JENI HAD BECOME GLORIA'S world, and nothing, not even life itself, could compare to the devotion she had for her little angel. So, when she received a call from the grade school principal that Jeni had been involved in an accident, Gloria's heart wrenched in horror. The principal assured Gloria that Jeni was fine and that he had notified Jim, who was on the way. However, the shaky tone and nervous inflection in the principal's voice, was not very reassuring, so Gloria bolted out the door nervously and drove immediately to the school.

Jim arrived first and found Jeni was safe with no obvious injuries, and after comforting her for several minutes, stepped into the hall for a minute to give his office a quick call to follow up on an important issue that had been interrupted by his unexpected and sudden departure.

"Where is she?" Gloria cried as she burst through the school doors.

"She's fine, Gloria." Jim quickly reassured her as he ushered his wife into the small school clinic. "Just a few scrapes and bruises— nothing serious."

"Jeni, sweetie, are you all right?" Gloria exclaimed, oblivious to everything and everyone in the room but her daughter. Wrapping her arms around her, Gloria squeezed so hard, it seemed for a moment to take Jeni's breath away.

After the initial panic had passed and Gloria was confident that Jeni was safe, she began to notice the people around her. There was Jim, the principal, Jeni's best friend Chloe, the school nurse along with another teacher she recognized, but who was the oddly dressed stranger? *He looks familiar,* she thought. *Where have I seen him before?*

"Mrs. Johnson," a voice interrupted her observations as she straightened up to address the speaker. "I am Felix Hernandez, and I just want to say how sorry I am for this incident and how grateful we all are that it was not more serious than it was." After this introduction, Principal Hernandez turned and took a step toward the stranger Gloria had been wondering about. "What is your name again?" he asked the stranger.

"Captain, but you can just call me 'Cap' for short, if you like," the stranger answered softly with a warm, gentle smile.

"Yes, Cap, that's it," the principal acknowledged, "well, it was quite fortunate, Mrs. Johnson, that Cap happened to be near Jeni at that critical moment to prevent the unthinkable."

Gloria started to shiver as Principal Hernandez related the story of Jeni's brush with death. Jim helped steady her as the principal continued.

"It would appear, as I have already explained to your husband, that soon after classes were dismissed, Jeni lost track of time while talking with her friend Chloe, and after suddenly realizing she was late for soccer practice, ran toward the soccer field. Without thinking, Jeni ran right between two busses directly in front of a car." Gloria's face turned white, as her mind raced from one horrifying scenario to another. The principal continued, turning to the Captain. "If it wasn't for this 'guardian angel' being in the right place at the right time, this minor incident . . . well . . . "

"It's all my fault, Mrs. Johnson," Chloe sobbed, her face red and wet with tears, revealing she had been distraught and crying feverishly for some time. Gloria turned to give her a reassuring hug.

"Don't give it another thought, dear," she said sympathetically while drawing her attention toward Jeni. "It wasn't your fault. See, Jeni's fine." Though her words were comforting to Chloe, they did little to comfort her own traumatized emotions.

Then Gloria turned her attention back to the stranger, and taking a firm grasp of his hands, tried to thank him with words she knew would never convey the deep gratitude in her heart. "You are an angel, an angel!" She finally said with tears, as her appreciation for what this stranger had done overpowered the uncomfortable eerie sense of familiarity that she had toward him. "An angel . . . "

"Mom," Jeni interrupted, "he is an . . . " Jeni's declaration of the Captain's identity, however, was cut short by a sudden pain as the Captain glanced over at her. Jeni bent over, grasping her side with a quiet moan as Gloria quickly left the Captain and flew to her daughter's side.

"What is it?" Gloria asked, anxiously.

"They did hit the curb pretty hard when Cap tackled her from in front of the car," Principal Hernandez added with concern.

"I'm sorry, I didn't notice anything more than a slight bruise when I first examined her," the nurse said a little defensively, while kneeling down to re-inspect Jeni's side. "I'm not sure what it could be, but I would advise a trip to the ER right away."

Gloria and Jim whole-heartedly agreed, and wanting Jeni to be professionally examined as soon as possible, said their goodbyes and thanked everyone for all their kindness and concern.

"How can we ever thank you?" Gloria said, stopping for a moment again to thank the Captain, on their way out the door.

"There's no need to thank me," He quietly answered, and then asked for a private word with her.

"I'm sorry, Gloria," the Captain began apologetically. "It wasn't my intention to meet your family this way, but as you can clearly see, circumstances required it."

"Should I know you?" Gloria asked, more than perplexed. "You seem so familiar to me."

"If you remember, we met briefly a long time ago," He said, "and we will meet again several years from now; although at that time, I'm afraid it won't have such a happy ending, at least at first."

He noticed Gloria's puzzled expression at this statement and related a story to help her understand.

"There was a dear loving mother a long time ago who had a son; and it was written about her in an ancient prophecy, *that her son would initially bring his mother great and abundant joy, but then a sword of sorrow would pierce her heart."* His face warmed with a look of compassion and then added, "You will not understand what this means at first, but eventually, through a friend, you will. Your heart will one day be pierced as that dear mother's heart was, but take courage. When that day comes, I will send a comforter who will give you hope, restore your joy, and give you peace."

Gloria was dumbfounded and couldn't speak. Her emotions had been spent, and she was exhausted from the day's events. However, when she looked up into the Captains eyes to say goodbye, that same unexplainable calmness came over her, and although still perplexed and confused, she was able to refocus on Jeni's immediate need.

Jeni also said goodbye to her friend, thanking him again for saving her life.

"I will always be there for you," the Captain assured her, as Jeni flinched a little at their embrace.

Cap gently touched her side as Jeni noticed an instant relief from the pain.

"You will feel better now," the Captain said softly as they parted.

"I've missed you, Cap, it's been so long. When will I see you again?"

"Soon, very soon. I promise."

Jeni looked back with an enduring smile and gave the stranger one last wave as they drove away.

"Do you both know this Captain person?" Jim asked, on the way to the ER.

"I'm not sure. He does seem a little familiar, but I can't place him," Gloria answered in deep thought, wishing she had an answer. "He said we met years ago."

"That's odd," Jim answered, and then added, "Do you think he's homeless?"

While Jeni's parents were preoccupied with their conversation in the front seat, Jeni was lost in her own thoughts. At one time Jeni believed Skeeta and Skoota were as real as her mom and dad. And, although they and others had long since departed from her imagination, she continued to see the Captain over the years. *It sure was strange to see him there today though*, Jeni thought.

"How are you feeling?" Gloria asked, turning back to Jeni.

"Amazingly well," Jeni answered. "I think he healed me."

"Healed you? Jeni's father asked suspiciously.

"Well, my side doesn't hurt anymore."

"You always did have a vivid imagination," Jim said with a laugh, "but I'm glad you're feeling better."

Jeni spoke no more of the Captain or the miraculous healing, as the three sped their way to the hospital. They did, however, rehash the day's nerve-wracking events, and couldn't help but speculate on several scenarios that were far worse than the one that ultimately played out.

Then, for no apparent reason, it started to dawn on Gloria who the Captain was. Memories started to filter into her mind, and then like a flood, burst into her mind like the brilliant rays of a new day. Unbelief overwhelmed her mind as she began to recall Jeni's odd description of her imaginary grown-up friend and the mysterious stranger that had visited them in that birthing room years ago right after Jeni was born.

Gloria and Jim had assumed the stranger was just another figment of Jeni's fertile imagination and that eventually he had gone the way of Skeeta ands Skoota; however, Gloria remembered Jeni had continued to 'imagine' the stranger; even after her other friends were long gone. She wanted to dismiss all this evidence, *but who else could it be? Is it even possible?*

"Jeni, is Cap, the make-believe stranger from your childhood?" Gloria asked, hoping to get a blank stare from her daughter.

Jim glanced at Gloria in astonishment. "Why on earth would you ask that?"

Gloria put her hand on his shoulder. Jim immediately noticed a perplexed and terrified look on her face.

"It was the Captain, Mama," Jeni answered matter-of-factly, "but he's not make-believe; he's real. I don't talk about him anymore because, well, you know, because you didn't like hearing about him."

Just as Jim started to protest the impossibility of such a preposterous thought, Jeni continued. "I'm not sure why he was at school today though. I've never seen him anywhere but at home before. I guess he was there to save my life. I'm sorry I caused so much trouble."

Gloria assured Jeni that they were just thankful she was all right, as Jim started to remember Skeeta and Skoota and Gloria's description of the odd man that visited her in the hospital right after Jeni was born.

It was difficult, to say the least, for Jim to accept Jeni's Captain as a real person, but the fact that this Captain had lingered in Jeni's imagination long after the others, as well as the multitude of undeniable evidences, compelled him to accept, at least in part, the remotest possibility.

Reflective silence pervaded the car as they pulled into the ER. For now speculations concerning the stranger's existence and true identity would have to wait.

After completing the usual admitting paperwork, the Johnson family was ushered into a small examination room. Under the care of the attending nurse, Jeni endured the predictable and generally mundane salvo of questions and the collection of vitals. After documenting the information, she kindly said her good-byes and wished them well, telling them the doctor would be with them very soon.

"Soon?" Gloria mused to Jim. She had had enough experience to know that a doctors understanding of the word 'soon', and Merriam-Webster's definition of the word were quite different.

Alone again, Gloria and Jim were able to continue contemplating the bewildering and strange events of the day.

"Jeni, honey," Jim began, trying to gain a better understanding of who, or what, this Captain person was, "are you saying that the man at school today is actually the same person you have told us about through the years?"

"Yes, Daddy, it was him all right, although it's been a while since I've even seen him. He doesn't visit as often as he used too."

"It isn't that we don't believe you, Jen sweet-heart," Gloria said with a sympathetic tone, "after all, we saw him ourselves today. It's just . . . well . . . seems too impossible to believe; that's all."

"I still don't believe it," Jim interjected skeptically.

"Still Jim, we can't deny he resembles in every way the stranger Jeni has talked about over the years. And he just happens to show up today to save Jeni's life? I remember him now, at the hospital when Jeni was born, and I am convinced he's the same man."

Jim's mind was reeling with doubt and confusion as he asked Jeni, "Tell us more about him . . . "

Just then there was a gentle knock at the door as it slowly opened. It was Dr. Michaels untimely appearance that belied Gloria's earlier musings of physician punctuality.

"How is everyone doing today?" Dr. Michaels asked, as he introduced himself and reviewed Jeni's information, as the trio acknowledged him in the affirmative.

"Mmmm . . ." he murmured to himself as he scanned the computer screen. "Mmmm . . . I don't see anything here to be overly concerned about," he said, motioning Jeni to the examination table. "Just jump on up here young lady, and let me have a look at you." Dr. Michaels said in jest, with a wink, knowing full well his patient was there for possible cracked or broken ribs. They all chuckled at the doctor's light-hearted joke when, to their surprise, Jeni did just that, jumped up on the examination table.

"Does this hurt?" the doctor asked as he gently prodded the supposed injured area.

Jeni responded negatively to each gentle push.

Mmmm . . . that's strange," he muttered to himself and then turned to Gloria and Jim with a questioning look. "Did you say she was hurt today? I can't find any evidence of trauma; I can't even find a bruise."

"We saw her double over in pain just before we left the school, and the nurse seemed very concerned; recommending we leave for the ER right away," Gloria confirmed.

"Mmmm . . . well, I don't understand it," the doctor again muttered to himself, looking quite perplexed. "But we better get an x-ray anyway just to be sure."

He called for a nurse to have Jeni prepped for radiology as he left the room, shaking his head. "This is very strange though, very strange."

"Strange?" Gloria said with a chuckle, after Dr. Michaels had left the room. "That doctor has no idea."

As astounding and perplexing as this day had already been, Jeni's radiology report was to add even more to the seemingly impossible revelations of the day. The report read: *'Subject had previously broken ribs along the third and fourth vertebra. Past injury appeared to be about three years old as indicated by scar tissue with proper healing observed. No immediate concerns or recommendations at this time.'*

10

Elle's World—Part 1: Moving on

ABOUT ONE YEAR BEFORE Jeni was born, Elle's husband Paul had succumbed to the ravages of cancer. He and Elle were *true soul mates* and their relationship was most envied. Of course they had had the usual skirmishes of differing opinions here and there and the occasional quarrel as to be expected, but these were mere bumps in the road, and not the devastating potholes and craters that many couples find themselves tripping over and falling into. Such was the rarity of Elle and Paul's love.

At Paul's funeral, Elle stood next to his casket as friends and family filed past. Through tears, she greeted each one with dignity and grace, thanking them for their support and honoring Paul with their presence. Senator Peters was one of the many people in line to pay his respects.

"Oh, Alan, how are you doing?" Elle asked, with a deep compassion that belied her own grief as they embraced. For a few moments at least, the consoled became the consoler.

"It's been hard as you know," Alan responded solemnly.

The long line of family, friends and colleagues waited as these two dear friends, for a few minutes at least, shared in their mutual grief and loss.

"They're gone," Elle said, shaking as her knees buckled under her. Fortunately, their embrace lingered long enough for Alan to stabilize her and keep her from collapsing completely to the floor.

"Yes . . . " Alan replied softly, as Elle regained her composure and strength.

Just a few weeks earlier, Elle had attended the funeral of Alan's wife. Both had lost their spouses within a brief month's time, and the heart-wrenching simultaneous losses of their friends and spouses seemed beyond bearing.

Alan and Paul were colleagues for many years and had become best friends, sharing similar hobbies, political views and other interests. Their wives also developed a very close friendship, as the foursome often frequented the finest establishments in town. Their lives were full and privileged; that is, until their illnesses. Then they were forced to exchange those finer places of status and pride, with ones better suited to accommodate the frailties and indignities of their ever darkening worlds.

"Let's keep in touch," Elle whispered before they parted, as Alan affirmed the suggestion with a light squeeze of her hand.

They did keep in touch occasionally and maintained a friendship that eventually blossomed into an intimate relationship uniquely their own.

"So, what do you think?" Alan asked, distracting Elle's distant thoughts.

"Well, I can't say that it's sudden after all this time," Elle responded, "but I must say it comes as a shock."

"Will you marry me?" Alan repeated again to solidify the suggestion in Elle's mind.

Until this question had been asked, Elle had no clear reason to confront the demons of her past or the cold stark reality of 'moving on'. Although, by all outward appearances she had adjusted well to Paul's passing, she had never truly taken the time to emotionally heal. *I haven't even opened Paul's letter yet,* she thought, as her eyes glazed over into a blank stare. Needless to say, Alan was dismayed.

Being the direct and bold person that she was, Elle thanked Alan for such a kind offer but knew she needed time to work through some neglected issues before entering into such an arrangement.

Although Alan initially felt the sting of rejection, and for a while some awkward moments occurred in their relationship, Elle eventually worked through the hard issues confronting her, and wedding plans were set in motion.

"Hey, Alan?" Elle asked, getting Alan's attention one morning before he left from his now-customary weekend visit. "You know how the girls and I get together every month for our 'Book Club', right? Well, I see on your schedule that you have a dentist appointment in town the same afternoon of our next meeting, and was wondering if you could swing by on your way home? I know Gloria and Frances would love to get to know you better. It would be so much fun if you could."

Although her friends knew of Alan through their relationship with Elle, and had met Alan in passing on a few occasions, their busy schedules hindered their natural ability to become more acquainted with him. So, when Elle's friends heard that they would be seeing Alan at their next meeting, there was an undercurrent of anticipation and excitement.

As the time of the meeting drew nearer, the giddy ladies felt they already knew Alan, from how often Elle had talked about him. On the other hand, Alan knew enough about Elle's friends to know that this meeting would be more like a formal question and answer session than a light-hearted get-together. Because of this, Alan affectionately began referring to the impending meeting as 'The Inquisition' to Elle's annoyance. Elle thought he was being silly, but Alan knew he would be outnumbered three-to-one with a gender that, on average, spoke a hundred words to one of their male counterparts.

"Now, Alan," Elle said, as Alan arrived after his dentist appointment, "no swearing today. You know Frances is sensitive and easily offended by that sort of thing. And don't talk about abortion, politics or anything. . ." Elle's voice trailed off as she went into the kitchen to turn off a light, and then continued without a break in her oration, ". . .and wear something casual, but not too casual, dressy, but not too dressy. Did you call the caterer and the minister as I asked? I hope it isn't too late to get the Olson Trio. Unfortunately, this is the prime wedding season and they are really in demand. Oh yes, we need to call and make reservations by the end of the day for the White House Banquet Hall, or we'll lose it."

Elle was just getting started; she was of the mind that if it was worth doing at all, it was worth doing perfectly. This wasn't her normal disposition, but on these stressful, special occasions, even Mr. Hyde wouldn't recognize her, and had hardly stopped to take a breath since Alan's arrival. Elle desperately wanted Alan to make a good first impression, but he could only shrink with dreaded apprehension at what it was going to be like having two more voices chiming in with Elle's, especially when their entire focus would be on him! *This truly will be an inquisition,* he thought.

After all of Elle's suggestions, warnings and commands had mercifully come to an end, they made their way to Frances' house.

"Alan, you look nice," Elle said before knocking on Frances's door. Alan was much relieved at this positive comment but still apprehensive to the awaiting panel of inquisitors behind the door.

The women were waiting eagerly to spend some quality time with Alan and lost no time inundating him with question after question, as they made themselves comfortable in the living room with coffee and snacks.

The afternoon wasn't as bad as Alan had built it up to be, and to his surprise, even relaxed and started enjoying himself. At one point the conversation went in the direction of having children. Frances' struggles and depression after the stillbirth of her child was one reason she and her friends continued to meet regularly after Paul's death; as they remembered and sympathized with Frances over this painful memory. Elle lamented her regret over never having any children and pointed to Jeni as an example of what she had missed.

"Jeni is such a sweet girl. We had such a fun time when she stayed with me the other day," Frances said, turning to Gloria. "You must be so proud of her."

"She's a little angel, for sure." Gloria confirmed, her face glowing with loving pride.

"No one would think twice about having children if they were all like her," Frances added.

"I hear that you have a religious background," Alan said, looking at Frances and abruptly changing the subject.

Although Elle had not specifically warned Alan against bringing up this particular subject, she was nevertheless shocked, as she glared at him for doing so. She immediately started damage control and did her best to divert the discussion but to no avail; the subject of religion had been birthed.

"By religious, do you mean am I a Christian?" Frances verified plainly.

"What's the difference?" Alan responded, solidly setting the conversation in motion.

"All Christians are religious, but not all religious people are Christians," Frances explained. "There is a difference between being a Christian and participating in religious activity. For instance, we girls meet 'religiously' once a month for our book club night, but it has nothing to do with God or spiritual matters . . . "

"Well, at least we try not to." Elle cut in sarcastically under her breath.

"A Christian is someone who desires a personal relationship with Jesus and believes what the Bible says about Him and what He did for us." Frances concluded, without loosing the flow of her thought, in spite of Elle's interruption.

"What did he do for us?" Alan asked with interest.

"He came to His creation from heaven, was born of a virgin named Mary in a little town called Bethlehem, and suffered and died on a brutal Roman cross, as a sacrifice for our sins, sins we had no ability to forgive ourselves."

"This is our safe place to laugh, cry, and just be real with each other," Gloria interjected, understanding the volatility of the current subject matter and wanting to diffuse the obvious tension in the room. "We started meeting weekly as a support for Elle after Paul's diagnosis, and then decided to continue meeting every month. It eventually developed into what we now call our book club."

"I personally don't get the church thing." Elle said, mockingly continuing the previous flow of the conversation. "I don't even know why people go to church at all; it's a waste of time. But I guess everyone needs a social outlet like a bar, or club, or something. To each their own, I say."

This last sarcastic statement from Elle seemed to bring the uncomfortable subject to a close. Alan was sincerely interested in pursuing the conversation further, but for Elle's sake, wisely decided to revisit the issue another time.

"As I look back," Alan reflected, desiring to restore a more pleasant atmosphere, "I would have appreciated a support group like yours when I lost my wife. You are very fortunate to have each other."

Every expression in the room, except Elle's, showed a sympathetic tenderness toward Alan at the mention of his dearly departed wife. Elle was still seething however over Alan's insensitive introduction of such a controversial and uncomfortable subject.

To Elle's relief, further controversial subjects were avoided, as the subject of religion, quickly drifted into other topics.

Alan, the centerpiece of this *inquisition*, not only came through unscathed and with a greater affection and appreciation for Elle's friends, but also a heightened curious interest in spiritual matters.

After the meeting and saying goodbye to Alan, Elle thought of another controversial issue that could no longer be delayed or avoided: The Letter . . .

11

Elle's World—Part 2: City of Stones

"There are cemeteries throughout the world, lifeless and cold places—memorials of lives that are no more. Birds sing their love songs in them, oblivious of its purpose, flowers bloom and wither with the seasons, as a plethora of animals and insects scurry above the now-silent hopes and dreams of so many once vibrant lives. Majestic trees of every shape and size tower over stone monuments; stones that have as much diversity as the cities and villages around them. Some are tall and magnificent, while others, simple and unpretentious. Many are neatly manicured, while others neglected, cracked and fallen—a sad epitaph for souls once pulsating with the vigor of love and life."

"So, the next time you walk by one of these Cities of Stones, as brother Jim calls them, ask yourself; are you longing for that heavenly home? Or, are you dreading the day when your flesh and bones lay cold in that City of Stones?"

"Oh, death, where is your sting? Oh, grave, where is your victory!"

(Excerpt from a sermon by Pastor Dennis—August 23)

Today, Elle found herself slowly walking past and between those many-shaped marble and granite stones. The same ones Gloria had lamented over those many years ago when bringing Jeni home from the hospital, and that Jim had dubbed, 'City of Stones'. The same one where Elle's beloved Paul was now resting.

Elle knew intellectually that one day, she too must eventually move from her earthly clay dwelling into one of these stone cities; but not on this brilliant sunny day. Today she was filled with the essence of life as she walked from one stone to the next, and over the many silent soul-less forms beneath her.

Then, stopping abruptly, a certain stone caught Elle's eye. She stood gazing at it for a second and then slowly walked over to it. She glided her hand gently over the chiseled contours of its shape and the beautifully engraved name, as she reverently knelt down in front of it. Alone with only her memories, Elle cried as she had not cried in years, still caressing its cold, hard surface.

After this first wave of sorrow had passed, Elle turned and sat back against the stone's smooth face onto the soft green grass. "I miss you, Paul," she whispered softly, as the reality of the fragility of life and the fear of the unknown gripped her soul. Emotions that had been pent up for far too long again burst forth with a vengeance, as she buried her face in her hands.

In her lap lay an envelope, now damp with tears. It was Paul's ominous letter, the one that over time had become a mysterious menacing idol-like shrine; and in her mind represented the last thread of connection to her beloved.

Sitting there with the beauty of God's creation all around her, and with a refreshing breeze cooling the warmth of the mid-day sun on her face, Elle's resolve to open Paul's letter waned. *Is it right to move on? Will reading this letter break the promise I made to love him forever? And what about the pain; will I have to relive that nightmare of grief all over again?*

But this was the day Elle had determined to face her demons and pour out, once and for all, the mysteries enshrined in its paper tomb.

By his singular question, Alan had unknowingly challenged Elle to confront and resolve the unsettled issues of her past. She also knew that if she was ever to embrace a new and wonderful future with him, this day, and its predictable pain, was an absolute necessity. Intellectually there was nothing to consider; Paul was gone and that was that. Yet, she knew what can seem so simple to the mind, can and often does, emotionally confuse and overwhelm the heart.

As she sat looking at the envelope through her tears, thoughts of betraying a sacred oath of eternal friendship clouded her mind. Memories of laughter, romance, and just being together began to emerge. Marriage vows of eternal devotion and commitment became fresh, though no longer having any connection with reality. The love she had for Paul, still buried in the depth of her soul, finally found vent, and her tears gushed forth again with a vengeance.

There was none to console her; Elle alone knew the deep sorrow in her heart. She was truly alone, alone as the silent lifeless forms around her. This overwhelming sense of loneliness was intensified by the fact that she had no hope beyond the grave. Someday she would be where Paul is now, here beneath her feet, and what then? *What then?*

Enough! She said to herself. *No more delays!* Confused and bewildered, Elle brushed away all the distracting and menacing thoughts, and with a defiant lifting of the chin, reaffirmed her commitment to do what needed to be done. So picking up the letter with trembling hands, and through a misty haze of tears, slowly began to peel back the flap of the ominous envelope. Once and for all, its hidden mysteries and secrets would finally be hidden no more.

12

Elle's World—Part 3: The Letter

ELLE CONTINUED TO GAZE at Paul's letter for what seemed like hours. She had turned it over and over again, touching one edge, and then the other, as if teasing herself as to whether she would open it or not. In her procrastination, she occasionally distracted herself by looking at the serene beauty around her. Majestic trees loomed over her, their branches thick with green leaves fluttering in the gentle breeze, as an array of white billowing clouds floated aimlessly by, framed in a sea of blue.

Finally, however, she found the courage to carefully peal back the seal. Her wet eyes shimmering in the sunlight, as she carefully removed the folded pages, freeing them at last from their prison.

As Elle drew out the folded pages, something fell to the ground and disappeared into the thick grass below her. After a few seconds of parting the long green blades with her fingers and frantically feeling for the item, she felt something hard and round nestled among the thick roots. It was a penny, just a simple penny . . . or was it? For how could an almost worthless penny cause Elle such a fresh outburst of emotion and tears?

Elle wiped away her tears so she could focus on the small print of the copper disk. As expected, the date on it was indeed her birth date. It was Paul's tradition to give Elle a penny with her birth date on it for every special occasion; and this was definitely one of those special occasions. She had nostalgically saved every one, and at home, had a drawer full of them. Elle mused with a sad melancholy as she glided her fingertip one last time over the date, before tucking it safely away in a pocket.

Returning her attention back to the letter, Elle unfolded its pages . . .

To my dearest Elle,

By now, if all has gone according to plan, I have been gone from your life for one year, and Pastor Dennis, following my instructions, has given you this letter along with my Bible, my precious and most treasured possession, and a book, The Case For Christ.

How I wish I could have stayed with you longer my love; but it wasn't meant to be. I also wish I would have had the chance to share with you, the new joy I found in someone who became very special to me at the end. His name is Jesus.

I love you with the deepest and truest love a man could ever have, which makes this imminent journey so much harder to bear. But God, in His mercy, has comforted me.

Elle, we have always said, 'seeing is believing,' but I have found a greater truth, that being, 'knowing is believing'. Facing death puts a perspective on life that can only be understood by the dying. This reality inspired me to, no, compelled me to look beyond this fragile life and face what was to come, if anything. I didn't want to take that final step over the coming threshold in ignorance; so, with Pastor Dennis's help, I began to seek beyond what I could see with these earthly eyes. . .

At this point, reflecting on the last weeks of Paul's life, Elle remembered a dramatic and unexplainable peace and calm in Paul that she couldn't explain or understand at the time.

She remembered how in the beginning, Paul was fiercely angry over his illness, and at one point even raised a clinched fist toward God in a fit of rage. '*God is heartless and cruel to treat humanity in such a vile way!*' he cried out, and then sneered at God's claim of being a 'good and loving God. '*A cold-blooded hypocrite is what he is, if he even exists at all!*'

She read on . . .

Knowing our shared and strong commitment to atheistic views, I knew it would add sorrow upon sorrow of unnecessary pain and emotional strain on you to add this betrayal of our long-held convictions at such a difficult time. . .

At this Elle lowered the letter, as again, a fresh cascade of tears began. Although she did not fully comprehend what Paul was trying to say in regards to his supposed betrayal, she did recognize within the loving sentiment, fresh memories of Paul's thoughtful, kind and tender nature. *To be so compassionate and understanding, as to think of my feelings, at a time when he was . . . was the one suffering and dying?* She continued reading . . .

I have not betrayed our love but fulfilled it, and raised it to a level higher than you could ever imagine!

So, though I was not willing to cause you grief at the time, it is my desire now to present to you the Good News of Jesus Christ and a love beyond human understanding. I want to share with you the reason for my loving betrayal, and present a case for this overwhelming new worldview of love, which I have embraced with all my heart!

Elle, by the will of God, he has made us the ultimate judge and sovereign ruler of our own path in this life. You can reject or accept what follows, but it is my earnest prayer and greatest hope, that my case is persuasive and sound.

"My Case for Christ"

"Vanity, vanity," the Bible says of this short life. It is a breath, a vapor, just a moment in an eternal sea of time. Look at all the celebrities, stars and millionaires that have flourished for a few years, and are now gone forever; dust! Gone where? You are a lawyer as I am. Prove me wrong. Examine the evidence as I did, and prove whether God is real. Is this life our true reality, or just a short fleeting dream?

It was my deepest desire to have the following song sung or read at my funeral, but again, I wanted to spare you the embarrassment of my newfound passion, so I would like to share it with you now . . .

"Don't Weep For Me"

Sooner or later it's time for us to go.
But, don't weep for me for I know where I'm to go.
For you see I've put my trust in the Creator's hands above,
So, when I go I go in peace to the Savior that I love.

Don't weep for me. Don't weep for me.
Cry for all those without hope,
Who stumble deep into the night,
Who haven't known the love of God or the mercy of His Light!
Don't weep for me. Don't weep for me.

Jesus is the Way the Truth the Life,
And if you call on Him you'll never die,
Call on Jesus now today, While there's time please don't delay,
To make Heaven your home, and where you'll never be alone!

Don't weep for me. Don't weep for me.
Cry for all those without hope,
Who stumble deep into the night,
Who haven't known the love of God or the mercy of His Light!
Don't weep for me. Don't weep for me.

Elle, this song reflects my sentiments and prayer for you and everyone that does not know the saving knowledge and love of Jesus Christ. It is my hope and prayer that time has softened your heart toward the idea that there might be a God, and the realization that it truly takes more faith to believe in the incoherent and random babblings of this world, than in the miraculously, perfectly ordered design of a Creator.

But if you are still not convinced, at least know that until the moment of my passing, I prayed earnestly for your soul! It is only now at this seemingly hopeless place of honest reflection, that I realize selfish arrogant pride alone keeps mankind from seeing the truth that is so obvious.

Did we bring anything into this world? Can we take anything from it? No, Elle, not even our great love could withstand the vice-like jaws of this cruel death.

I plead with you to invest the time to seek out the evidence of creation and not blindly follow the culture of our age. Review the secular evidence to confirm historical and archeological records of consistency that parallel the biblical record. Along with my Bible, I left a book Frances gave me entitled, "The Case for Christ" by Lee Strobel. His research is sound and convincing. Also, read the Gospel of John with an open mind to hear what he has to say about the Word of Truth and may you receive the Lord of all comfort, and be with Him always.

I hope and pray that this letter does not offend you or taint the memory of our love, for I love you with an everlasting love, and will go on loving you beyond my last breath. For me, the grief of our part-ing will soon be laid to rest, but you Elle, my dearest Elle, must live on to love again.

Don't weep for me, but if you have yet to know the forgiveness of Almighty God, weep for yourself. And, don't be bitter with those who implore you to accept the loving gift of Jesus Christ as I am now, for the motive of their loving entreaties is sincere, and made with the deepest compassion for your eternal soul.

Farewell then my dearest, and I hope to see you one day here with me in God's wonderful Paradise, so our love and friendship can continue on forever and ever.

With all my love,
Paul

Alone, and surrounded by both beauty and death, Elle lowered the letter and looked anxiously around as a flurry of thoughts invaded her mind. The content of the letter was not at all what she had ex-pected. She didn't feel betrayed, but neither was she deeply moved by Paul's appeals. Her emotions were extreme and polarized at the same time. There was the predictable reawakening of a deep sorrow that she had expected by the stirring of suppressed memories, yet there was also a relief in knowing Paul had found some semblance of peace and comfort in those last days as well.

Carefully refolding the letter, Elle placed it back into the tear-stained envelope. She was reminded of the intellect, practical wisdom and logical thinking that she so admired and respected in Paul. This fact made it hard to merely brush the letter off as a dying man's folly, no matter how bizarre and out of character it seemed. The other thing that haunted her was Paul's radical change in those last weeks. *Is there a God?* She thought. *Could Paul be right? After all,* she mused, *who wouldn't want to believe in a happily-forever-after fairytale when death finally comes knocking at the door?*

Elle dried her tears and stood to stretch, brushing the leaves and grass from her clothes. She walked away from that City of Stones with a lighter heart that day. The spell of Paul's mysterious ominous letter had finally been broken, never to haunt her again . . . or would it?

13

Gloria's World

"Mom! What happened?" Jeni yelled, terrified as she ran into the kitchen after hearing a loud crash. "Are you all right?"

Upon entering the kitchen, Jeni discovered Gloria bent over, one hand clinging to the edge of the sink and the other to her side. A dish had shattered, spreading broken fragments across the floor.

Jeni knew right away what had happened: her mom was having another attack of that merciless side pain. Not only had this relentless pain continued over the years, but had become more frequent and severe.

"What can I do to help?" Jeni asked as she ran barefoot to her mother, oblivious to the hazard on the floor.

"Don't come in here with your bare . . . !" Gloria started to warn, but it was too late.

Jeni's foot recoiled involuntarily as she felt a sharp pain. Then, almost losing her balance, she hopped on one leg the rest of the way into her mother's arms.

It was then Gloria's turn to recoil and reel from a new pain shooting up her leg, as she thoughtlessly stepped forward to catch Jeni. They both stood helpless now, each standing on one leg and looking like a pair of flamingos.

Dismayed, Jeni asked, "Now what will we do?" The pair gazed at the glass shards surrounding them.

"Well, there is one thing you can do," Gloria grimaced, still doubled over in pain. "Tell me I'm not crazy like all the doctors say I. . ." Gloria winced, as another jabbing pain caused her to grab her side. "I'm not so sure your dad isn't starting to believe it as well," she added in frustration.

"Don't say that, Mom . . . "

Just then Jim came home, and being drawn by the commotion in the kitchen, assessed the situation and immediately carried the two injured 'flamingos' safely over the sea of glass into the living room. After examining their wounds and determining that they weren't as severe as first thought, Jim treated and bandaged his girls with the utmost gentleness and care. He gave each an affectionate kiss and then headed off to the kitchen to do some serious cleaning, and to prepare supper for the two invalids.

"How are my two precious girls doing?" Jim asked, returning a short time later. Then, addressing Gloria, he asked, "and how is your side, dear? Was it the cause of all this?"

"Yes, but not as much as my foot does at this moment," Gloria jested.

"I'm so sorry, honey," Jim said, sympathetically offering another comforting kiss before returning to the kitchen.

"See, Mom," Jeni said, reassuringly, "you're not crazy."

"I know, sweetie, I'm sorry. That was just my worn out frustrated nerves getting the better of me."

"It must be terrible having to continually endure that pain," Jeni said, echoing her father's lament, as she gave her mom a sympathetic hug and kiss of her own, "especially since it was my fault."

"Your fault?" Gloria reacted astonished that Jeni would think such a thing.

"But Mom," Jeni insisted, "didn't these pains start when I was born?"

"Oh, Jeni, that's nonsense!" Gloria said, while affectionately combing her fingers gently through Jeni's soft black curls. "I know it seems that way, but you're not to blame."

Jeni did, however, have a good reason to be suspicious of her mother's condition being related to her birth. She had overheard on more than one occasion, her parents and others mention that there was a connection, or at the very least, an eerie coincidence between the two events.

Almost eighteen years had passed without a cure, or even a diagnosis. The doctors had long since exhausted every possible cause, as hope, now barely a glowing ember, seemed to be extinguished forever. It seemed there was nothing left for Gloria to do but to accept patiently this relentless persistent pain, maybe even for the remainder of her life.

"Mom, I've been thinking, especially now, with what just happened. I think I should stay home from college and help you here."

"What?" Gloria responded with a gentle reprimand in her voice. "No sweetheart, everything is set for you to go, and you've been preparing and looking forward to college for such a long time." Then, with a playful gesture pointed to their bandaged feet, added, "Besides, it appears your dad will be taking great care of me while you're away."

"He is a pretty special guy," Jeni agreed with a look of pride and endearment sparkling in her eyes.

"You don't know the half of it," Gloria said, taking Jeni's hand. "It hasn't always been this way, you know." Gloria paused and then added, "I've never told you just how special he really is, have I?"

"No, I mean, I don't think so," Jeni said, questioningly.

"Well, it's about time I did," Gloria said, with another affectionate caress of Jeni's hair. "Now, to understand how special your father is, you first need to understand how wretched I was to him when we first got married; we almost didn't make it."

"You, Mom?" Jeni asked, dumbfounded at the remotest possibility.

"Well," Gloria began, "it is true, but I thank God it hasn't been true for a long time. You see, growing up, I had some serious issues that caused me to treat your dad, well, I won't sugarcoat it—shamefully. To be honest, I wasn't even sure that I loved your father when we were married, which made things even worse."

"Not love Dad?" Jeni responded in disbelief. "He's amazing! But, if you didn't love him, why did you marry him?"

"Well, it is a little hard to explain, or to even understand, but ultimately, it was an unhealthy need for attention, and a need to feel safe, that compelled me to marry your father."

"What happened? You seem great together now." Jeni paused, and then asked with a slight fear of apprehension, "You *are* doing great, right?"

Gloria suppressed a chuckle and squeezed Jeni's hand reassuringly, as she realized her confession, was causing Jeni some anxiety. "Oh, honey, no worries there, what I'm telling you happened long before you were born, and your dad and I love each other, now more than ever."

Jeni relaxed and breathed out a sigh of relief.

"You see, Jeni," Gloria said, returning to her narrative, "I was raised in a home where there was no love or affection, at least outwardly; no hugs, no affirming words, not even an occasional *I love you!*"

"What!" Jeni exclaimed, surprised. "Were Grandma and Grandpa really that way when you were growing up?"

"Unfortunately yes, and as a result, getting attention was my first and foremost objective in everything I put my mind to. I had to be the best at everything, and the center of attention; if not, I was nothing. For me, rejection was the worst feeling in the world, and because of that, insecurity and neediness led me into all sorts of trouble, especially unhealthy relationships."

Gloria thought of a conversation she had had with her father, causing her to suppress a chuckle.

"What's so funny?" Jeni asked, confused as to how her mom could laugh while telling such a heartbreaking story.

Gloria could feel a belly laugh coming on and burst out hysterically, "It isn't funny, and that's what makes it so funny!" Gloria said, again trying in vain to restrain herself, and producing an embarrassing snort for her effort.

"What is it? Tell me!" Jeni pleaded, wanting to be let in on the joke.

Through tears of laughter, now mingling with the earlier tears of pain, Gloria explained how one day she asked her dad why he had never said '*I love you*' to her. "Oh, Jeni, you would have thought the world had come to an end, from the shock on Grandpa's face. He denied it completely of course, and then went on to explain how absolutely wrong I was. *Why that's not true at all*, he said indignantly, *remember that time I took you to the store and gave you a choice between the talking doll and the dress-up doll?* With that, he promptly dropped the uncomfortable subject and walked away."

It was now Jeni's turn to attempt restraining her own mirth at such a silly response, as she tried to rein in her own incredulous emotional snort of suppressed laughter. "That, that . . . is so sad," Jeni attempted to say, as the irony of the thought, made them both erupt all the more into a paroxysm of all-out laughter.

"Was Grandpa really that mean?" Jeni finally asked, after regaining a semblance of composure. "I was too young to remember him."

"No, not at all, as I learned when I got older. Your grandpa would have given the shirt off his back to help us kids, or anyone else for that matter. No, in time, I realized Grandpa just wasn't comfortable showing affection; it was just his way.

"But Grandma hugs all the time!"

"I'm getting to that part," Gloria said, attempting to suppress another involuntary spasm of laughter.

"What is it this time?" Jeni insisted.

"Oh, just wait until you hear this one," Gloria responded, again with a muffled snort. "Something happened years ago that changed everything for Grandma!"

"What?" Jeni persisted again, as Gloria started in on her new narrative.

"Well, years ago, when your dad and I were visiting Grandma and Grandpa; I walked by Grandma in the kitchen, and for some reason, it came into my head to give her a big bear hug, the first in my life that I could remember."

"What happened?" Jeni asked, wide-eyed with curiosity.

"Oh my stars," Gloria continued with animation, "I'm not kidding, her reaction was so violent, and so involuntary, that when she pushed me away, I stumbled and almost hit my head on the edge of the table behind me!"

"No way!" Jeni reacted in astonishment. "But Grandma hugs everybody, now!"

"She does now," Gloria responded. "I'm not exactly sure what triggered the change in her after that first hug, but a few months later, I noticed that Grandma was hugging everyone, and had became the *huggiest* person in the world."

"She sure is," Jeni agreed.

"Well," Gloria said, continuing to sum up the point of her two sad, but comical stories, "because growing up without affection was so painful, and because of the many negative ways I sought to fill that void, I resolved that one day when I had a family of my own, I would smother my children with all the hugs, kisses and *I love you's* that I could!"

"And, you sure have, Mom, and I love it!" Jeni said, grabbing her mom around the neck and giving her a big hug. "I couldn't imagine growing up any other way."

"Yes, but like I said, it wasn't always this way. How your father put up with me, heaven only knows. Your dad had the patience of a saint, and what seems like a limitless well of forgiveness.

"Maybe it's because Dad grew up going to church," Jeni suggested.

"Maybe," Gloria reflected," all I know is that I'm glad he is who he is, and that over time I grew madly in love with him."

"I'm glad too."

Just then, Jeni noticed a sad change in her mother's expression. "What?"

"My insecurities and selfishness hurt you as well." Gloria admitted sadly.

"How?" Jeni inquired.

"Because, it was my choice that kept you from having a sister or a brother, at least here with us. It seemed so right at the time, though your father was so adamantly against it, but, . . . " Gloria hesitated for an instant, obviously emotionally moved with sadness and regret. "Jeni, my selfish choice, kept us from having more children."

"Forget it, Mom," Jeni quickly responded, perceiving a past abortion, had triggered the reason for her mom's distress. "What's past is past, and what's done is done," Jeni stated energetically, trying to dissuade her mom's regretful melancholy mood.

Jeni's effort was not in vain, as Gloria looked up with a fresh glow on her face, and a smile that seemed to restore her color. "When I first held you in my arms, it was the most wonderful experience of my life! The very moment I looked into your eyes, I realized just how foolish I had been to think that such a beautiful and amazing gift, could ever be considered an inconvenience."

Now it was Jeni's turn to tear-up, as Gloria and Jeni sat arm in arm with a fresh and new awareness that their relationship had wondrously transformed and changed from mother and daughter, to the best of friends.

"What's this?" Jim asked concerned, entering the living room to check on his girls and seeing the recently shed traces of tears. "Are you both still in that much pain?"

Ignoring her father's question, Jeni jumped up, as best she could on her flamingo leg, and threw her arms around her father's neck. "I love you, Daddy," she whispered tenderly into his ear, as he gave Gloria a questioning glance.

Gloria's unspoken look when their eyes met told him that their little girl wasn't so little anymore, and that Jeni, leaving for college in just a few short months, would leave behind a sad emptiness that would change their lives forever.

14

Til Death Do Us Part

MANY YEARS HAD PASSED since the Captain had made an appearance; in fact, his visits had stopped right after the school incident. With such a long absence, time had virtually put him out of everyone's mind, except Jeni's of course. She still longed for his companionship and missed him greatly. At first Gloria and Jim were very concerned and curious over first hearing about, and then actually meeting the Captain, but as time went on with no additional appearances, their memory of him had slowly faded into obscurity, and was seldom thought of, or mentioned.

One beautiful, mild late autumn day, Gloria lazily reclined in her favorite chair against a soft comfortable pillow, reading one of her favorite books. A gentle breeze filtered through one of the open windows near her, distracting her for a moment, as she looked out at the few remaining leaves fluttering erratically, and still clinging stubbornly to their branches. The ringing of her phone however, interrupted her self-indulgent tranquil afternoon.

"Mom, I think I'm in love!" a voice burst out on the other end, not even giving Gloria a chance to say hello. "His name is Michael, and he is such an amazing guy!"

Jeni was in her second year of nursing school, with a Medical Transcription elective, being one of her goals; and though there had been an occasional mention of 'love' interests in her day-to-day communications with her mom, none had generated this kind of excitement.

"We met at the library!"

Gloria could tell immediately by the unique passion in Jeni's voice, that this Michael, whoever he was, was the real deal. "When can we meet him?" Gloria pressed Jeni impatiently.

"Soon, Mom, very soon," Jeni said excitedly. "You'll love him!"

Plans were made for the first visit, and Michael eventually became a frequent guest at the Johnson home.

Michael was working through a first-year medical internship but still hadn't decided for sure what direction he would ultimately choose for his vocation. He was an only child, and his parents lived in the suburbs of a small city near the college. He was tall, a little gangly for Jeni's taste, but she figured some consistent home-cooked meals would fill him out just fine. He dressed neatly, even for casual events, and was always a respectful gentleman.

Now it is true that anyone can make a good first impression; Gloria knew that better than most, but time proved that Michael was authentic. As Gloria and Jim grew to love him as the son he was destined to become.

The following summer Jeni found herself out on a small dinghy on a secluded lake drifting lazily along, enjoying the cool breeze of a warm summer day. This was well out of the ordinary, because Jeni and Michael usually spent their time studying at the library where they met, or going to one of the parks near campus to relax. This day, however, was special, and Jeni knew it. She was convinced it was the day that almost every young girl, in their childhood imagination, dreams of.

The day started as any other day with the rituals and routines common to everyday life. School had ended for the year, but there were always the electives to keep them busy, not to mention Michael had committed to finishing his studies as quickly as possible, so he and Jeni could get on with their lives together. This left the pair very little time for lounging and dreaming. Today, however, was an obvious departure from their normal routine, and when routines are interrupted, there can be an unbalancing effect on the emotions. So it was with Jeni.

Although it seemed her childhood fantasy was about to come true, Michael's sudden departure from the predictable caused apprehension and anxiety to nag at her. Then the memory of a young girl named Anne from *Anne of Green Gables*, who thought she was in love for two years only to discover she wasn't in love at all, gave her another reason to pause.

Am I truly in love? Jeni thought reflectively. Jeni knew that doubts had a way of creeping in when expectations shift unexpectedly, and the events of this day were truly unexpected. *What will I say if . . . or how will I respond if . . . ?*

The first thing that was out of the ordinary was the fact that Michael showed up at Jeni's apartment with his car instead of his bicycle. They often enjoyed riding the local bike path around the lake and stopped frequently at the various parks along the way. They enjoyed the different concession stands and always discovered something new on these adventures. There were jugglers, pets of all kinds doing cute tricks or chasing a ball, venders with a myriad of different items to sell, flying Frisbees, and musicians, crooning out songs from days gone by had their guitar cases open, hoping for appreciative listeners to throw in a few bucks for their effort.

The next thing Jeni noticed was that Michael avoided direct questions and was acting suspiciously. He seemed undeterred however, and moved forward with whatever he had planned, in spite of Jeni's persistent and nagging questions.

On their way, she then noticed that Michael was driving in an unfamiliar direction. They usually took the freeway when visiting either his parents or hers, but this country road they were on was unknown to Jeni.

After penetrating deeper and deeper into the rural countryside of woods and farmland for about an hour, Jeni's patience began to wear thin. She was about ready to release an unpleasant torrent of pent up frustration, when Michael turned down a long private driveway flanked on either side by dense woods. The gravel driveway was lined with tall mature live oaks that spread like a canopy over their heads, and down each side was a well-kept split rail fence, with flowers, shrubs and small evergreen trees planted for their greatest artistic effect.

Due to the length and claustrophobic nature of the tree-lined path, Jeni's anxiety began to revive. Then, an old, rustic log cabin emerged from behind some trees, with a lone figure standing on the porch waving at them.

"Chloe? Is that you, Chloe?" Jeni called out the window as they pulled up to the old, but immaculately kept cabin. She threw open the door and ran to the porch with her arms open wide, as the two lifelong friends embraced enthusiastically.

"It seems like ages since we've seen each other!" Chloe cried out excitedly.

"It does; what a surprise!" Jeni said, after catching her breath. "But, I don't understand."

"Ask your chauffer," Chloe said with a glance in Michael's direction.

Entering a different field of study than Jeni, Chloe had moved to a college in a different state to further her education; so of late, these dear lifelong friends seldom had an opportunity to see each other. For Jeni, this made Michael's surprise all the more wonderful, though somewhat more baffling.

"What are you doing here?" Jeni asked, perplexed. Then, upon reflection, she rephrased and reemphasized her own question. "For that matter, what am I doing here?"

Chloe explained that this was her parents' vacation home, and when Michael found out it came with its own private lake, asked if he could surprise Jeni with this special, out-of-the-ordinary day.

"I didn't even know your family had a vacation home," Jeni said, still somewhat bewildered by all the unexpected events of the day.

"It was one of our rental properties that had been in the family for generations, until a few months ago," Chloe explained. "My parents decided it would make a great vacation home; so here we are."

"Remember when we went to visit Chloe a couple months ago and went out for pizza?" Michael said, turning to Jeni. "Chloe just happened to mention the cabin when you stepped away to get a drink or something, and I asked her to keep it a secret so I could surprise you."

"Well, I'm surprised all right," Jeni blushed.

"A vacation home with its own lake is pretty cool," Chloe commented, as Jeni requested a tour.

"Well, let's save the tour for later," Michael suggested, interrupting Jeni's request reluctantly. "We have a date on the lake just now."

Later Chloe explained that 'Lake Marion' was named after her great grandmother, or possibly one of her great aunts; no one really knew for sure. She was a young girl about Jeni's age, and was proposed to in a rowboat on that very lake about one hundred years earlier. Michael had heard of Chloe's research on the history of the little lake, and thought it would be great to imitate Marion's romantic day with Jeni.

As the two embarked on their lake adventure, Jeni felt a little underdressed for such a special occasion, and at the same time, a little overdressed for an excursion on a lake in a rowboat. But neither Jeni nor Michael thought much of their apparel; their minds were on the significance of that day and what it would mean to them for the rest of their lives.

It was a beautiful bright summer day with just enough clouds to give a little relief from the sun's warm rays streaming down on them, and then allowing them to pop out again briefly, to chase away the cool chill of the lake air.

Jeni and Michael's day was as beautiful and romantic as could be imagined; with the exception of Michael's occasional boyish pranks of rocking the boat, or warning Jeni frantically of a dangerous poisonous snake, which would turn out to be just a harmless waterlogged branch floating in the water.

"What is that?" Jeni pointed in wonderment, as they drifted past a small toy boat floating in the water with Jeni's name on it.

Under Michael's direction, Chloe had launched this small vessel into an alcove near the house for them to 'eventually' find.

As Jeni picked up the little boat, its roof shifted a little, revealing a small velvety blue box inside. As Jeni reached in to retrieve and open it, Michael, unbalanced by the rocking boat, clumsily fell to one knee.

"Jeni, I would be so honored if you would be my wife. Will you marry me?"

At that moment the dingy drifted from under the shade of an overhanging bow, allowing the brilliant rays of the sun to dance and sparkle through the many facets of the tiny precious stone Jeni held in her hand. "Oh, Michael, it's beautiful!"

The awe of the moment and the radiant beauty of the colorful glowing diamond so mesmerized Jeni that she overlooked for a minute the question that had accompanied the dazzling gem.

"Oh, oh yes, yes of course I will, Michael!" Jeni finally cried, as Michael took the ring and placed it on her finger.

As he looked into her eyes, he saw they were moist and shimmering in the sunlight; even more radiant and beautiful than the ring she was now wearing. Then, after an affectionate embrace, they headed for shore.

Docking the boat, they made their way to the cabin, where a grand celebration feast that Chloe had prepared was waiting for them.

"Well, was it as wonderful as you hoped it would be?" Chloe asked, seeing by their expressions there was really no need to ask.

"Yes, it was so romantic," Jeni answered, lifted her hand to show off her new engagement ring. Michael wasn't immune to the joy of the moment either, as he beamed from ear to ear.

Chloe's romantic candlelight dinner of smoked salmon, fresh broccoli, buttered garlic-mashed potatoes and fruit salad was appreciated, delicious and memorable.

Gloria and Jim, as well as Chloe, were soon helping with the wedding plans, and enjoying it almost as much as Jeni and Michael were; especially Jim, who found endless ways to apply his unique creativity to the event. The year flew by quickly, and with only a few days to spare, were finally ready.

"No regrets?" Michael asked solemnly one night, as he and Jeni sat together after a full day of preparations.

"Not in the least!" Jeni answered confidently. "You are the most kind and gentle man I've ever known, except for Dad of course, the truest, true love of my heart!"

"I had an unnerving dream last night that you were going away and never coming back," Michael said, with a tremor of fear in his voice. "It seemed so real."

"Nonsense!" Jeni quipped back. "It was just a silly dream. I'm not going anywhere!" She said, giving Michael a reassuring kiss, and then with a reaffirming smile, added, "I think you're stuck with me for a long, long time."

As Michael shared his dream, Jeni reflected on her own from the night before, as she looked into Michael's worried eyes. *Or was it a dream?* It had been so long since the Captain had visited, that she doubted her senses. *Was it real?* Jeni knew that it was, but her new practical adult mind struggled against her childhood memories. All she knew for sure, was the Captain had visited her that very night, while in a half-asleep dreamlike state.

"It's time for you to come home now, my sweet princess," the Captain announced, with a gentle kiss to her forehead, and then vanished.

I can't share my dream with Michael, Jeni thought, as she could clearly see Michael's continued anxiety over his own unnerving dream; *I've never even told Michael about the Captain.* She tried to brush it off as nothing, but the Captain's visit continued to haunt her right up to the day of their wedding.

Jeni and Michael's special day had finally arrived, as a flurry of last-minute details were checked and rechecked. The church aisle was graced with a velvety white rice-paper runner covered with fragrant flower petals randomly scattered down its length, and each pew adorned with color coordinated bouquets of flowers and ribbons. Jeni's wedding dress was beautiful, and would have been the envy of any princess, while the bridesmaids, in their matching dresses and groomsmen in their long-tailed tuxes, were all ready to go.

Gloria sat in the front row next to the main aisle, with Frances, Tom, Elle and Alan. Michael waited impatiently for his precious bride's grand entrance, as they all turned and looked with anticipation as the processional began.

A few of Jeni's very young cousins were the first to march down the isle with rose petals, from their ribbon-covered baskets, being flung in every direction but where instructed. In contrast to this flamboyant trio of girls, a stiff and petrified 4-year-old nephew of Michael's followed, his eyes glued to his singular task with the utmost concentration. He held a small ornamentally embroidered pillow with two rings securely tied to it with a silk ribbon. Down the aisle he marched like a trooper on parade, as a hundred guests aimed their cameras and phones for just the right shot. He was terrified, and although he did arrive at the appointed destination, accomplishing his important mission to the great relief of many, it was plain to see that he longed to be anywhere, but where he was.

Then, Chloe, Jeni's bridesmaid, made her entrance. She was as radiant and beautiful as the bride herself, with one of Michael's brothers as best man by her side. All was ready. Jeni made her grand entrance with her father and took her place next to Michael.

The service was traditional; the message on point, and all was going well and according to plan until the vows were to commence. Gloria, very familiar with the symptoms of her persistent attacks, felt a tinge of pain pulsate through her body, the dreadful foretelling of the onslaught to come.

No! Not now! Gloria groaned, as she determined with all her might, not to let this attack spoil her daughter's wedding. But what started as a slight ache, quickly turned into a shooting pain, which caused her to double over and collapse into the aisle at Jeni's feet. Those gathered gave a gasp of surprise, as an inexpressibly stabbing pain seized Gloria.

Why now, of all days, why today? Gloria lamented in a fetal position on the floor, as she cringed under the most severe pain she had experienced to date.

Gloria was nearly unconscious, when she felt someone grab her arm. It was Jeni, with a look of horror on her face. As Jeni's hands clenched tighter and tighter, Gloria realized something was wrong, and that something, or someone, was trying to drag Jeni away from her. Seeing the terror in her daughter's eyes, and in spite of her weakness, Gloria involuntarily grabbed Jeni with both hands, in a desperate attempt to hold her close. Jeni's incessant cries for help reawakened Gloria from her stupor, just long enough to make one last frantic attempt to save her daughter from whatever this mysterious and unknown force was! But there was no remaining strength.

"Mama! Mama! Don't let them take me! Mama . . . " Gloria heard Jeni scream in terrified anguish, as their hands were finally ripped apart under the power of this unknown antagonist. Now exhausted, and having succumbed to this violent struggle and excruciating pain, Gloria lay as dead, unconscious on the floor.

15

A Mother's Lament

Dazed and disoriented, Gloria reluctantly emerged from her mental fog, as an intense feeling of dread, came over her. As she became more aware of her surroundings and the circumstances that landed her in the hospital, she noticed the pain that had caused her collapse was gone. In her half-conscious state, she fumbled clumsily under the covers to feel her side. *How strange*, she thought, *no bandages; not even a Band-Aid!* After a quick survey of her condition, Gloria could find no evidence that a procedure had even been performed. *How long had she been out? Did they do a non-invasive procedure to stop the pain?* She wondered, as she drifted off into a sleep-like haze again.

"Jim, is that you?" Gloria inquired sheepishly, still in a dazed stupor, as a jarring of the bed reawakened her. A shadowy figure passed by the bed as Gloria strained to bring her eyes into focus, but to no avail. She was still at the mercy of the anesthetic's lingering effects in the dimly lit room.

"No dear, it's Kate, your nurse. Lay still and rest for a while. There was a slight complication with the procedure, but nothing to worry about; everything's just fine."

After the nurse left, Gloria dosed off again, until a familiar voice softly called her name.

"Gloria? "

"Jim, is that you?" Gloria asked excitedly.

"I'm here. The nurse said I could wake you now," Jim said softly, as he lovingly squeezed Gloria's hand lightly. "Everything is okay, but you will need to rest a little longer before we can go home."

"I feel better than I have in a long time," Gloria said with amazement, yet still with that unexplainable, ominous cloud of gloom hanging over her.

"Yes, they were able to find the problem and stop the bleeding."

This is amazing, Gloria thought, as she again stretched and twisted slightly to test for any lingering pain that she was all too familiar with. *All this time, it was because of some bleeding issue?*

Then suddenly, she remembered the wedding and Jeni's cries for help. "Jim! Where's Jeni! What happened after. . . after I fainted? Are Jeni and Michael married? Where is she?"

"Jenny? Wedding?" Jim asked, confused and alarmed. "Who's Jenny? What wedding . . . ?"

Just then the nurse walked in and saw Gloria's agitation. "Gloria, you need to calm down and rest," she said, putting a comforting hand on Gloria's shoulder. "We'll be back in a few minutes to check on you."

"Don't be alarmed, Jim," Kate said reassuringly, as they stepped into the hall away from Gloria's hearing. "Disorientation is fairly common when patients wake up. Let's give her a little time to clear her head, and then she should be herself again."

Alone again, Gloria still felt that unexplainable anxious dread hovering over her. She strained to bring her eyes into focus, curious at her unexpected surroundings; and the more she observed, the more perplexed she became.

This is not a hospital recovery room, she thought, as that anxious dread loomed even more menacing. *Where am I?*

There were the familiar magazine racks on the wall with a variety of reading materials, along with posters displaying cross-sections of human anatomy, typical in many doctors' offices, but then, Gloria noticed a poster on the wall that read, *'Your Rights as a Woman'.*

Strange. Why would I be in a recovery room with a poster like that?

Then she saw another poster entitled, *'The Choice is Yours'*, followed by words that belied her reason, *'Poster provided by Planned Parenthood'*. The overwhelming dread that Gloria had been feeling now darkened with an even more ominous horror, as the reality of where she was, gripped her heart, even to the depth of her soul. She shook with fear and trembling.

This is not a hospital, its . . . its an abortion clinic, Gloria shuddered at the thought, and then with all her will power pushed it away from her mind as Jim reentered the room.

"Jim, where am I?" Gloria pleaded nervously as she grabbed his arm. "Where's Jeni? How was the wedding? Where's Michael? Is everything okay? I'm so embarrassed—I ruined everything!" Jim tried to speak, but Gloria pressed on, "Where are they? I want to see them now!" A sense of terror now rushed through her, as she gazed wide-eyed into the eyes of her perplexed and bewildered husband. That looming menacing dread, crushed down about her furiously, as if a cloudburst of rain, lightning and thunder were unleashed simultaneously. Tears started to involuntarily flow, as she pleaded again for her child. "Jim, where's our Jeni?" she groaned. "Where is my baby . . . ?"

Exhausted and now fully aware of how terrible the embarrassing scene of her collapse at the wedding must have been, Gloria continued to lament her regret, grief and despair to Jim. However, when she looked up at him through her tears, expecting comfort, and an answer to her many pleas and laments, all that met her eyes was a contorted, confused dumbfounded look.

"Jim, what's the matter?" Gloria cried in dismay. "Has anything happened to them? Why was Jeni pulled from my arms? Why do you have that look on your face?"

"Gloria," Jim said softly, holding her hand and responding as gently and calmly as possible to her laments. "I'm sorry, dear. I don't know what you're talking about, or even who you're talking about." He moved closer and began to caress her hair, as was his custom when Gloria was excited or stressed. "I don't know a Jenny or a Michael or anything about a wedding."

Gloria's mind was in a torment of confusion, as she tried to make sense of what seemed impossible. How could she believe any reality other than the one she had just lived?

To comfort his distressed wife, Jim repeated what the nurse said about the lingering affects of anesthesia, and how it can momentarily cause disorientation, but there was no help for the truth that was settling upon her.

She strived and succeeded for only a brief moment, to push back the unthinkable thoughts of this new reality, but it was as though a stampede of wild animals was approaching from a distance and getting closer and closer, and louder and louder. Her mind floated between denial and acceptance. Confused, she wanted to escape, but to where? She wanted go back to the church and the wedding; but was there even a church or wedding to go back to?

What is real? Is this a nightmare? If I fall back to sleep, will Jeni be here by my side when I wake up? Will I ever see Jeni again? All Gloria knew, dream or not, was that she wanted to leave this horrid place and go home. *Maybe when I get home she'll be there waiting for me* she thought in her forced delusion.

"Do you remember my note?" Jim asked tenderly, interrupting Gloria's thoughts.

That simple question jolted Gloria's mind into an unshakable reality, as she bolted up with a start, and quickly felt in her pocket for the note Jim had left her. It was there, '*I beg of you, don't do this . . .* '

Gloria's mind was spent. It was all so clear now, as she looked around one more time at the posters on the walls and Jim's contorted and confused face. This nightmare in fact, was her reality—there was no more denying it. The charging stampede was now upon her, thundering unmercifully through her head. The undeniable truth had grasped her mind like a gazelle caught without mercy in the clutches of a ravenous lion. There was no more hope, no mental escape remaining, and in the midst and finality of this hellish and horrifying truth, Gloria burst out with an agonizing scream that could be heard throughout the entire facility. Her heart-wrenching screams of loss and regret seemed to emanate from the mournful pit of hell itself. What Gloria didn't know however, was that her cries and laments were being heard, and together with Jeni's soul, were being ushered through the gates of Heaven at that very moment, into the very throne-room and loving heart of God.

"Jeni! Where's my Jeni? Jeni! Where's my baby?" Gloria screamed hysterically over and over again, as she buried her face in her hands between her knees, shaking and trembling.

"What have I done? What have I done?" she cried over and over, in a torment of grief and tears. She was inconsolable. Jim tried to comfort her, but every attempt to calm her with a gentle touch, was met with flailing arms.

"Don't touch me!" She screamed, and then buried her face again between her knees in convulsive wailing and tears. Her anguish seemed like death itself. She wanted to die. Her soul was dead, cold and lifeless.

"Nurse!" The doctor yelled sharply from the hallway. "You need to calm that woman down, or we'll have another incident to report, not to mention the negative publicity!"

"Gloria, you have to settle down right now, or you will rupture and start bleeding again!" The nurse exclaimed excitedly after the doctor's reproof.

Now both mentally and physically exhausted from all that had taken place, Gloria finally began to welcome Jim's gentle and loving caresses, as she rocked back and forth in his arms. "Where's my Jeni? She lamented again, this time quietly and reflectively. "What have they done with her? Oh, my baby," she muttered to herself. "I want to hold her just one last time. Oh, my beautiful, beautiful baby . . ."

Gloria had a lifetime of regret to ponder, as Jeni's entire life passed before her, as she sat sobbing in Jim's arms, *Jeni's birth, Skeeta and Skoota, her first day of school, Chloe, Michael*. With all these thoughts, a fresh flood of tears poured down her face as she looked up at Jim. "Our Jeni will never marry Michael, will she?" After saying this, she dropped, as though lifeless, into Jim's compassionate arms.

When the final papers for her release were signed, Gloria asked if she could see her baby. "Can I take her home?" she asked, wanting to both be near her as well as give her a proper burial.

The receptionist answered in no uncertain terms that it was impossible. "It just isn't done, and strictly against policy to allow anything of the sort," she said, emphatically. Then flippantly she added, "You wouldn't want to see her, ah, I mean, what's left of the tissue, anyway."

How cold, Gloria thought, *how could she become so numb to what I see now as such a barbaric and evil thing?* The receptionist, however, wasn't without some feeling or humanity, as she volunteered a small bit of information that Gloria would treasure in her heart forever.

"A girl?" Gloria repeated overwhelmed, as her knees buckled under her. Jim and the nurse helped her into a nearby wheelchair as they made their way to the car. *A girl child,* she repeated quietly, *my child . . . my little baby girl . . . my Jeni . . .*

The journey home was deathly quiet, as Gloria eerily observed the same graveyard she had commented about in her dream, though only hours ago, still had a sense she had made it many years ago. However, this time, she did not have the same distain and loathing of it. Now she had a desire to honor Jeni, with her own place of eternal rest and remembrance.

As the blur of houses and street signs passed by, Gloria reminisced about Jeni and the events of her dream. *How will I ever find forgiveness for what I've done? It is unforgivable*, she lamented, a swelling anger starting to rage within her as she thought of the poster in the clinic. *My right to choose?* She sneered sarcastically; *it wasn't my choice! It wasn't my right! I was wrong. . . so, so very wrong!*

Still bewildered and puzzled at Gloria's outburst of emotion, Jim still had no idea of the cause, but he also knew, because of Gloria's state of mind, that he would need to wait for a more favorable opportunity to unravel the mystery of Gloria's grief. So, as they made their way home, Gloria mourned in silence, and Jim waited patiently for an answer to this mystery.

16

What Is Truth?

GLORIA KNEW SHE OWED Jim, who was against her having the abortion in the first place, an explanation for her bizarre behavior at the clinic. So, a few hours after returning home and through many tears of regret and shame, she related Jeni's story to him, as he graciously and sympathetically listened and comforted her.

A few days later, although the weather was bright and cheerful outside, a cloud of gloom and mystery hovered over her friends as they waited breathlessly for the revealing of Gloria's lament. The day had finally come to put all the rumors and gossip to rest, as Gloria was now ready to confide to her friends the deep pain in her heart.

"I know it was just a dream," Gloria began to explain, "but it was so real! You were all in it, even Paul and Alan. It was like reliving our same life together, but with, with my Jeni. . ." Gloria looked away as the mention of her never-to-be daughter's name reactivated the pain of loss that was still so fresh.

Gloria dried her tears, realizing as never before how much she appreciated her friends. They had become like sisters, and now, with the love and gentleness of sisters, they comforted her.

"Jeni is real," Frances said softly, after the initial storm of Gloria's pain had passed.

"What is the big deal?" Elle chimed in, trying to lighten the mood. "After all, these procedures are common and done every day. I haven't heard anyone else complain over having one; besides, it's a free choice under the law." To Elle, law was everything, and everything she believed filtered through it.

"I know, Elle," Gloria said, in response to her appeal. "I did make this choice of my own free will, and for reasons that seemed so right at the time, but now . . . " Gloria looked away again to hide her face. "I don't understand how something that seemed so right just a few days ago could now seem so wrong."

"Because it wasn't wrong," Elle reiterated with emphasis, trying to bolster her lawful position and hoping Gloria would return to her senses and be relieved of this unnecessary pain and guilt. Elle's sincere desire to convince Gloria that she had done nothing wrong was authentic and appreciated, but wasn't very effective.

"But Elle, once our eyes are open to the truth, we cannot become blind again," Frances explained, trying to show why Gloria's conscience could never be comforted and withdraw back into her previous blind ignorance. "Once truth has entered a conscience, it can't be ignored. Truth can be rejected, but never altered."

"Truth?" Elle retorted sarcastically. "What is Truth? Truth is what we make it!"

Fearing a continued dialog in this direction would start an argument and cause Gloria unnecessary grief upon grief, Frances diverted the conversation back to the loving care of her friend.

"You're not alone in this, Gloria. We love you like a sister and will be here for you as long as you need us." Elle concurred with sympathetic agreement. Meanwhile Frances pondered a more opportune time to share with Gloria, the Hope and Salvation that would truly and miraculously bring a permanent peace to her mind and soul.

Gloria was indeed comforted by the love and fellowship of her friends, as a glimmer of hope broke through the gloomy cloud hanging over the room that day. However, after parting from her friends, and finding herself alone again in her solitude, the thought of what could have been, and even more terrifying, what should have been, returned to haunt Gloria.

"So, you really want to do this?" Jim asked Gloria consolingly.

"Yes, I know my dream wasn't real, but Jeni was!" Gloria said with conviction. "If I hadn't made the choice I made, Jeni would be in my arms right now!" Gloria paused with moistening eyes at that thought, and then added soberly, "Maybe even living that very life I dreamed."

Gloria again reflected on the fact that there would never be a Michael in Jeni's life, as she turned to Jim. "Jim, I believe she was a real person, as real as you and I. I believe she had a soul, with her own unique personality, and that she was truly our daughter. I believe that as much as I have ever believed anything. I can't explain it, but it's as if, even now, Jeni and I share a deep bond of love that only a mother and child can truly experience or know."

Jim drew Gloria close as he pulled a handkerchief from his pocket to dry Gloria's tears.

"I was wrong. I was so very wrong to take Jeni's life from her," Gloria continued to lament. "So the least I, or we can do, is to honor her in this small way."

"I agree," Jim responded sympathetically. "I know you need this; we both do," he said with a loving embrace. "I will call tomorrow and make the arrangement."

A few weeks later, Gloria and Jim walked through the Crest Point Cemetery, where plans had been made for little Jeni to be laid to rest on the one-year anniversary of her death. Gloria remembered the many times she had passed these stones, and loathed them for the dreadful death they represented. But now she realized the importance of honoring the loss of someone so dearly loved. She realized that Jim's 'City of Stones' wasn't to be feared as much as appreciated; a place where goodbyes could be made, and the occasional hello revisited. In this brief moment of reflection, as Gloria stood in the midst of death, a feeling of peace came over her, and for the first time this City of Stones didn't feel so depressing and fearful, but almost serene and beautiful.

"The service will only be symbolic," Jim mentioned as they turned to leave. "The little casket will be empty."

"I know. . ." Gloria started to respond, but then turned to Jim after a moment of reflection and said, "No, no it won't be empty, Jim. Our love will be in there; and her memory. We can visit her often and dream about how our lives might have been, as each year goes by."

Life settled back into its routine as Gloria tried to allow the passage of time to distance her from the sad memories and regrets of her past. She found, however, that time didn't heal all wounds, especially those of a lonely broken heart wracked with guilt and despair. The past could not be altered. Time, she realized, did not have the power to bring her pain to a merciful end, but instead was a daily reminder of it. If law and time was not the answer for this relentless grief, what was?

Therefore Pilate said to Him, "So you are a King?" Jesus answered, "You say correctly that I am a King. For this I have been born, and for this I have come into the world, to testify to the Truth. Everyone who is of the Truth hears my voice." Pilate said, "What is truth?" And when he had said this, went out again to the Jews and said to them, "I find no guilt in Him." John 18: 37–38

17

The Captain Revealed

"ALAN, YOU WOULDN'T BELIEVE the guilt and remorse poor Gloria is going through over a simple abortion," Elle said one morning just before heading for the office. "Women have a right to do what they want with their own bodies and that should be it!"

"It is the law," Alan agreed, matter-of-factly.

"It is the law," Elle reemphasized passionately. "I don't understand why people grieve over such insignificant things. There was no more life in that child than the child in her dream!"

"Child?" Alan mused, amazed at Elle's gaffe.

"Oh no, see!" Elle sneered, with a wave of her hand in a gesture of frustration. "They even have me talking nonsense over the whole thing!"

As Elle struggled with her conscience, Gloria was meeting with Frances to find comfort for her own.

"Frances, you seem to know more about what I'm going through than anyone else," Gloria said, making herself comfortable in Frances's living room. Frances prepared coffee and a few appetizers for her guest, thrilled to finally have an opportunity to share the hope and forgiveness of Christ with her hurting friend.

"Thank you so much for inviting me over," Gloria said gratefully, as she took a sip of coffee. "I didn't know where else to turn. I know how painful it was when you lost your baby a few years ago. How did you get through it? What makes you so strong?"

"Oh, I'm not worthy of such praise," Frances responded humbly. "There's a Wisdom and Strength far greater than mine that has done the work." Frances thought for a moment, and then continued. "You know, Gloria, at first I turned my rage and hate toward God, and even Tom, but then, I surrendered it all to Jesus. If I hadn't done that, things would have turned out very differently."

Frances related the sad story of her child's stillborn birth and the resulting separation and almost divorce from her husband, Tom.

"The sadness and guilt consumed my life."

Gloria thought back and remembered the remarkable change that had taken place in Frances several months after her loss. She remembered something Frances had shared, but Gloria and Elle never did fully understand what she was talking about or what actually brought about the change. All they really knew for sure, was at that time, Frances became the religious fanatic that she was today.

What was that saying you told Elle and I years ago?" Frances asked. "It was something like, if you believe God, you would live different? Or, something like that anyway."

"I remember," Frances responded. "How could I forget? It goes like this, if I believe in Jesus, and the Gospel is true, would I still live the way I do? It was a clarifying thought that if I truly believe in what I believe, it would just be plain foolish to go on living like my faith wasn't real or true."

"Wow, if that wisdom and strength can help me as much as it has you, Frances, I'm ready to listen," Gloria admitted with eager anticipation. "I have a pit of loneliness inside so deep, I can hardly bear it; I can't shake the guilt no matter what I do!"

"I know," Frances responded compassionately, as she put a comforting hand on Gloria's knee.

"Everyone has been so concerned and helpful, but I'm still so miserable and lonely. Is there any hope for me? Is there something you can do that will ease this regret and shame that's breaking my heart?"

"Gloria," Frances said with tenderness, "there's nothing I can do, but if you like, I will introduce you to the one I know who will give your soul the peace and rest it longs for."

"Is that Someone Jesus?" Gloria asked, having witnessed enough of Frances's life to assume as much.

"You know it is," Frances confirmed, giving Gloria an encouraging radiant smile.

Frances went on to share the rich, forgiving love of Jesus Christ, the truth of the Gospel and how the convicting truth of that thought, years ago, helped reveal how shallow and powerless her Christian life was.

"So, because Jesus died on a cross," Gloria interjected, to clarify what Frances was sharing with her, "we can be forgiven of everything we've ever done and be reconciled back to God; even after what I did to Jeni?"

"Yes—absolutely!" Frances answered confidently. "Jesus' gift of the cross took away all our sin, from the biggest to the smallest, from the first to the last; and all you need to do is accept that Gift."

"But even if I accept His forgiveness, how will I ever forgive myself?" Gloria asked, in hopeless despair.

"Forgiving others, or even ourselves, is impossible without God's help and strength," Frances answered. "It is because Jesus forgave us, that we have the power to forgive others as well as ourselves."

"I'm sorry, Frances, I don't mean to be rude, and I truly appreciate your help, but I still don't quite understand."

"No problem," Frances responded, "Let's try this. It says in John 3:16, *For God so loved the world that He gave His only begotten Son that whosoever believeth on Him should not perish, but have everlasting life.*"

Frances allowed Gloria to consider the familiar Bible verse for a moment, and then said, "The important thing to remember for now, is that Jesus, the Creator of all things, loves you so much that He died for you, and that all you have to do is believe and accept Him freely."

Gloria gazed at Frances with a puzzled look. "But, can it be that simple? Just believe?"

"Just believe," Frances echoed, reassuringly.

"It all sounds so wonderful, Frances," Gloria said, starting to realize a glimmer of hope at the thought. "But who is this Jesus anyway? I've only heard His name as a swear word most of my life." Gloria blushed a little at this statement, as it was more of a confession than an observation, but Frances, for Gloria's sake, focused on the question.

"It says in the book of Daniel," Frances began, picking up her Bible from the coffee table, "that Jesus came from the Mountain of God without hands, that is to say, He is not a created being, nor just a human, and not even an angel. He is a mountain to Himself, independent, but absolutely fully God. Sometimes I refer to Him as, *a chip off the old block.*"

The girls laughed at the thought of the old one-liner, and then Frances continued.

"Gloria, in pride we choose to rebel against God to fulfill our own selfish desires. Because of that rebellion, we became sinners and are separated us from his Holiness. Only by being transformed back into holiness can we again live in the presence of God; and only through Jesus' death on the cross, can this transformation be possible! *'For God so loved the world He gave . . . '* was God's provision. *'That whosoever believeth on Him . . . '* is our privilege to accept that provision."

Frances handed Gloria the Bible. "The best way to get to know Jesus and to understand how we can be forgiven, in spite of our sinfulness, is to read His Word. You can have this one; all you need to know is in here."

"Thank you so much, Gloria responded, appreciatively. "But, if Jesus died on a cross." She continued innocently. "Isn't He still dead?"

"Oh, no, Gloria, not at all. He is alive! Jesus rose from the dead three days after His crucifixion; that is why we have such a great hope in Him. He promises to raise us from the dead as well! It says in John 11:25-26, *I am the resurrection and the life; he who believes in me will live even if he dies, and everyone who lives and believes in me will never die. Do you believe this?'* That is why I am convinced that Jeni is alive today and with Jesus, right now!"

"Alive! Jeni, Alive!" Gloria reacted, stunned.

"Yes, I am convinced she is alive, and with Jesus, as we speak."

With this new hope, Gloria hung on every word as Frances, in Bible study-like fashion, went on to share more of the love of Jesus with Gloria; His birth, His names, some of His miracles and claims, even non-Christian historical accounts of the crucified carpenter from Galilee.

"In the New Testament, as you already know, He is known as Jesus or Jesus the Christ," Frances pointed out. "A few of His other names are Emanuel, which means 'God with us'; the Messiah, which means 'Savior', the Son of Man and the Lamb of God. In the Old Testament, He is known as the Lord of Hosts, the Root of Jesse, the Captain of the Hosts . . . "

"Wait, wait!" Gloria interrupted, wide-eyed and astonished. "Captain? Did you say Captain?" She exclaimed, hardly believing what she had just heard.

"What is it, Gloria? "Are you all right?"

"Show me where it talks about Jesus being a Captain."

"Sure, I'll look it up, but are you okay?" Frances asked again, wondering what could have caused such a reaction.

After a brief search, Frances found the passage in the fifth chapter of Joshua and pointed to it. "I'll start reading here from the thirteenth verse . . .

"And it came to pass, when Joshua was in Jericho, that he lifted up his eyes and looked, and, behold there stood a Man over against him with His sword drawn in His hand; and said unto Him, art thou for us, or for our adversaries? And He said, Nay; but as Captain of the host of the Lord am, I now come. And Joshua fell on his face to the earth, and did worship, and said unto Him, What saith my Lord unto His servant? And the Captain of the Lord's host said unto Joshua, loose thy shoe from off your foot; for the place whereon thou standest is holy. And Joshua did so."

Gloria was speechless, and Frances wanted to know why.

18

Not Alone

"WHAT IS IT?" AN impatient Frances inquired, curious at Gloria's reaction to what she had just read. Bewildered, Gloria sat stone-faced, trying to reconcile this bizarre revelation to her dream.

"Remember the stranger I told you about in my dream?" Gloria finally started to explain. "I never mentioned his name, but it was Captain, or Cap, for short, and I think there's a connection between the Captain in my dream, and the Captain you just read about."

Frances immediately realized the significance of this new information. "When you described him the other day as a stranger, I thought it might have been a guardian angel or something; but Jesus? Now it's all starting to make sense. Your Jeni's Captain was Jesus!"

"What is starting to make sense?" A mystified Gloria questioned.

"The fact that Jesus was there with Jeni, comforting her at the end!"

"You mean that . . . that, Jesus . . . ?" Gloria's eyes widened, as she started to comprehend the merciful vision Frances was painting.

"Gloria, the other day, when you said the stranger continued to make his presence known, even after Jeni's make-believe friends had all gone, and then later, at the school, I knew he was sent from God. But I didn't know exactly his significance, or that it could have actually been Jesus."

"If only that were true!" Gloria considered, thoughtfully, "If only . . . "

"It is true, and you can be sure of it," Frances said emphatically, hoping to instill Gloria with new confidence. "You see, it wasn't just a dream; it was God's way of letting you know that, in spite of what you were doing, He loves you, and cares for you, and to show you that Jeni was not alone; He was there with her the whole time!"

The first glimmer of lasting hope since that dreadful day started to settle upon Gloria's soul. *If what Frances is saying is true,* she thought, *then Jeni is not only still alive, but safe and happy. Could it be true!*

While Frances allowed this new sense of hope to soothe Gloria's tired mind, Gloria became curious about this Biblical Captain. "How do you know the 'Captain' you read about in the Bible is Jesus, and not an angel or something else?" Gloria asked, curiously.

"Well, there are many characteristics that identify God throughout the Bible, but in the Old Testament, there are two in particular," Frances began to explain. "One is the fact that whenever God shows Himself to someone, the ground around him is holy, and the other is that only God, not angels, will accept worship. The fact that this 'Captain of the Hosts' both told Joshua to remove his shoes because he was standing on 'holy ground', and the fact that he accepted worship, proves it had to be Jesus, not an angel."

"Frances, in my dream, this Captain, Jesus, told me about a mother, having great joy over her child, but then was pierced through the heart. He said a friend of mine would one day help me to understand. Do you know what he meant? Do you know who he was talking about or how it relates to me?"

"Yes, Gloria, that is so amazing. He was actually talking about His own mother, and you."

"His own mother? Me?"

"Yes, you see when Jesus was born, His mother Mary knew the baby she held in her arms was very special, because she was a virgin when she conceived, and she was also told, by an angel, he was the Messiah. This filled her heart with great joy, but then, when she saw Him tortured, crucified and brutally killed, her heart was pierced through with a great sorrow."

"Then, even in my dream he knew how much I would come to love Jeni, and how a sword of regret would pierce my own heart." Gloria's eyes filled with tears. "My heart has been pierced, just like he said!"

Before they parted that day, Frances comforted Gloria with many reassuring words and reminded her of the love and forgiveness that could be hers in Jesus, if she would only ask.

A few days later, Frances received a call very early in the morning from an excited Gloria. "I have something amazing to tell you!" she said impatiently. "When can I come over?"

"Right now!" Frances responded, without thinking.

A few minutes later, Gloria was at Frances's door.

"Can I get you anything?"

" No, no, no, I'm too excited for that! Maybe later."

"What is it?" Frances asked, starting to get a little concerned. "Are you all right?"

"Oh yes, yes, I'm fine! Never better!" Gloria reassured Frances. "It's just that . . . I . . . I think I'm what you Christians call, saved."

Frances hadn't seen Gloria this radiant since she had had her abortion, and rejoiced at the life-changing news, and peace.

"Frances, all I know," Gloria started to explain, trying to catch her breath, "is that everything you said about Jesus is true, and that my little Jeni, is with him right now!"

"When, where, how did all this . . . ?"

"Believe it or not," Gloria interrupted, with a laugh, "another dream?"

"Another dream?" Frances questioned, noting the irony. "Tell me all about it, while I get us some coffee."

"Well, Frances," Gloria, began, "the dream went like this . . .

I was in a courtroom, standing in front of a very tall bench, with a big white-bearded old Judge with fiery eyes, looking down at me. Suddenly, the courtroom became a flurry of activity, as the Judge commanded, "Bring in the witnesses!"

An attendant opened a door, as hundreds, if not thousands of people, started to file into the courtroom. A well-dressed man, near the bench talking to the Judge and pointing first at me, and then at the people coming through the door, seemed to really upset the Judge and make him irritated.

Then, to my surprise, I started to recognize a few of the witnesses; a teacher I had made fun of in grade school and an old department store employer I had once stolen a shirt from. I recognized others; friends, family, and then the courtroom went deathly quiet, as a young girl ran through the door. With big sad questioning eyes, she looked curiously around the room, searching for something or someone, until our eyes met. Then instantly, her face brightened with a warm loving smile.

"Mom?" She asked with excitement, as she ran to me. "Is that you?"

At that instant, I recognized my Jeni, all grown up, a young girl; and in shock, I fainted and collapsed as though dead, to the floor.

"Mommy, I forgive you, I forgive you," Jeni said pleadingly, as she knelt down by my side. She threw her arms around me, as loving tears started to fall from her eyes.

A moment later, I heard another voice.

"I forgive you too, my daughter." The soft gentle voice said, as He lifted me to my feet. It was the Captain, I mean Jesus. The moment he touched me; a peace I'd never experienced in my life, came over me. And as soon as he said I was forgiven, the well-dressed man that had been arguing with the judge turned and sneered in disgust and rage at me, while all the witnesses started exiting the courtroom. For a moment I was frightened, but then he left with the others, as the room became quiet and almost deserted again.

"Where are your accusers?" Jesus inquired, with gratification.

"They've, they've all gone, sir," I answered in astonishment.

"Neither do I condemn you. Go in peace."

"I love you Mama, but I have to go now." Jeni said, with a kiss, as she tenderly threw her arms once more around my neck, "We will see each other again soon though, so very soon."

I gave my darling baby one last lingering hug, before she ran from my sight, as the attendant closed the door behind her.

To my surprise, I wasn't crying. The euphoria I felt at that moment was. . . was well, unbelievable, and even more unexplainable! I *woke up, knowing I had accepted, at some point during the night, not only Jesus' complete forgiveness; but also, him as my Savior."*

Frances was speechless once again.

"Frances, the guilt is gone!" Gloria continued, beaming from ear to ear. "I understand now! I am truly forgiven! Everything is forgiven; even what I did to. . .!" As Jeni's name entered Gloria's mind again, a fresh sense of loss caused a brief sadness to show on her face. Even wrapped in the forgiving arms of God's love, Gloria felt the sting of Jeni's absence.

"I know," Frances, said compassionately, taking Gloria's hand. "God's forgiveness doesn't always take away the memories of what our sin has cost us, just the guilt and shame of it."

"Well, there is one thing I know," Gloria, sighed with relief, as she wiped away the remaining tears from her eyes, "although I abandoned Jeni, Jesus never did, and never will. Jeni is not alone; I know that now with all my heart. Jeni is not alone."

19

Final Goodbyes

THE NEXT GATHERING OF the girls was tense and uncomfortable to say the least. What started as a loving resource to comfort Elle through a painful chapter in her life had become an intolerable situation, where Elle felt like an outsider. Her dearest friends shared a passion that she, for the present, had chosen to reject; in spite of the clear evidence of her friends' enriched and peace-filled lives. They were bound together by an unseen and unknown rival that Elle didn't understand and stubbornly refused to accept. In her mind, religion was still a crutch for the weak, a lie or at best, a myth. So, in spite of Paul's pleas from beyond the grave, and her friends' kind and loving coaxing, Elle continued to reject this common bond shared by her friends.

"Alan, what am I to do?" Elle complained one morning in despair, hoping he could shed some light on her dilemma. "They have been my best friends for years; yet, ever since Gloria's abortion, everything has changed!"

"Well, they are what they are, and you are what you are, there's no changing that," Alan said, clearly seeing the inevitable shipwreck on the horizon as he sought safer ground. "The only thing to do now is to respect each other's views, and move on the best you can."

"What about you?" Elle asked, unconvinced and not in the least consoled by Alan's suggestion.

"Well, I'm not so sure about the God thing," Alan volunteered hesitantly, with as much honesty as he felt comfortable expressing at the moment. "But I will say, after hearing Gloria's story, it might be a good idea to reconsider our view on abortion."

"What?" Elle responded incredulously. "First Frances, the Jesus freak, then Gloria, and now you?"

The agitation in Elle's voice escalated, as Alan recoiled with an involuntary step backward.

"I have had it with all of you guys!" Elle cried, as she went through the house venting her rage, both at Alan and the world.

"You guys?" Alan questioned, defensively and confused. "So, I don't have a right to express my own opin . . . "

"All you morally superior people can just go to . . . !" Elle screamed, interrupting Alan with no few expletives.

At this point, Elle turned her back on Alan, muttered a few more inaudible expletives, and marched away through the kitchen, slamming cupboard doors on her way.

Alan had never seen Elle this out-of-control and wasn't exactly sure how to respond, but before he had a moment to think, Elle returned to continue her rant.

"First, it's God this, then Jesus that, and now you, of all people. You! You're considering changing a fundamental view that we've both shared ever since we've known each other! So now what? You are against women and their rights? You want to throw us all back into the dark ages?"

Alan made a futile attempt to reason with Elle, but all it did was agitate her into a greater temper.

"I suppose you'll be joining Frances's little church choir before long!" she screamed, with the most incredulous disrespect and sarcasm she could muster, slamming the bedroom door between them, effectively shutting Alan out. "Just go away! Go away!" Alan heard through the door.

Elle's rage was spent, as only muffled sobs now could be heard through the door. Alan's heart wanted to console her, but his mind knew better than to intrude on Elle's space while she was in this highly emotional state. All he could do was wait.

Little did Elle know, as she wept that day alone in her bedroom, that within a few short weeks, her relationship with Alan and her closest friends would be strained to the breaking point; and in fact, would break, never to be made right again. Her misplaced belief that she had been rejected and betrayed by her friends was far from the truth, nevertheless, in the rich soil of bitterness and unforgiveness, her resentment festered and grew more intense over time, until there was nothing left. Resentment and self-pity were Elle's closest companions now, and she clung tightly to them until the very end.

In stark contrast to the lonely despair into which Elle had descended, a peace and joy beyond understanding were springing up and growing brighter in Gloria each day. As Elle had sarcastically predicted, Alan did indeed start attending Dennis's church, but to the relief of everyone who knew just how vocally pitch-impaired he was, mercifully chose not to join the choir.

Proudly and without fear or excuse, Alan began to defend the defenseless in the senate chamber and be an advocate for the countless unborn children whose lives were daily being destroyed. He worked tirelessly to change the laws, and to stop the judicial support of 'sanctioned' institutions that encouraged what he considered to be medieval debased and barbaric practices of child abuse and sacrifice.

"Look." Gloria said to Frances as they walked through Jim's 'City of Stones' the following spring. She was drawing Frances's attention to one particular gravesite. Gloria had come to terms with what she had done, and had found an authentic peace and forgiveness through the transforming power of the blood of Christ. No longer did she dread the 'City of Stones' that she once feared and despised so vehemently. Nor would she fear for her own sake, when it was her time to take up residence within its walls; for she now had a hope and a vision beyond its lifeless hold. *Oh death, where is your sting? Oh grave, where is your victory,* a sweet voice echoed in her mind.

As Frances looked to where Gloria was pointing, she saw Paul's gravestone.

"I sure miss Elle," Frances said nostalgically as Paul's stone reminded her of the pain and loss of Elle's friendship. "Did we push her away?" She asked, putting her hand gently on its chiseled edge.

"No, Frances," Gloria answered consolingly. "It was her choice. We chose to believe and honor God, while she chose a path away from Him. We didn't reject her; she rejected us. . . and God."

The melancholy mood that had settled upon them soon vanished into the clear, azure sky above with its cotton like clouds, as they refocused their attention on the purpose of the day. This was Jeni's day, a special day to honor her, on this first anniversary of her death.

Friends and loved ones had all gathered on this lush, well-manicured grassy lawn to pay their respects, and to celebrate the life of this precious child, a soul, that had been conceived and had flourished with life for just a few short months; never seeing the light of day, but alive as any other living soul that has ever lived.

Alan was there with Jim and Tom, along with several members of Dennis's church, and other family and friends. They were all there to commemorate Jeni's precious life.

Grateful to be finally honoring her in death, as she had not in life, Gloria took one last look at Jeni's little casket, before turning away. Jeni's dream-life, once again, flashed through her memory, comforted by the lyrics Elle had shared with her months earlier from Paul's letter.

> *"Don't weep for me, don't weep for me.*
> *Cry for all those without hope,*
> *Who stumble deep into the night,*
> *Who haven't known the love of God,*
> *Or the mercy of His Light.*
> *But, don't weep for me, don't weep for me . . ."*

"It's amazing how much Jeni accomplished in her short life," Frances whispered to Gloria after the service. "I think she may have accomplished more in those short three months inside of you, than most people accomplish in a lifetime; and maybe more than if she had lived to be a hundred years old!"

"That is such a precious thought, thank you," Gloria responded, turning to Frances. "It seems almost as if God sent my little angel on a special mission. Through her, I was saved, Jim, Alan, and who knows how many others?"

After the ceremony had concluded, Gloria and Frances walked again past Paul's stone, as Gloria pondered how valuable and precious Frances's praise of Jeni's life had been. *What a beautiful thought . . .*

"By the way, Frances," Gloria said mischievously, with a flush of crimson radiating from her face. "I'm not showing yet, but Jeni will soon have a little sister, and in honor of what Jesus has done for me, and for so many others, Jim and I have decided to name her, Grace . . . "

Jeni Ann Johnson

Beloved daughter of Jim and Gloria Johnson
Abiding forever in the loving arms of her Captain

Conceived May 18th 2018
Died August 21st 2018

EPILOGUE

An Innocent Cry

MY MOTHER'S CRITICAL JOURNEY of loss and redemption led her into the precious, forgiving, and loving arms of Jesus Christ; my Stranger friend, the Captain. And because of this, my mother and I will once again be reunited, forever to enjoy the perfect splendor of heaven together.

In Genesis 50:20 Joseph said to his brothers, 'You intended to harm me, but God intended it for good to accomplish what is now being done, *the saving of many lives.*'

As in Joseph's case, God took my mother's misguided decision to harm me, and turned it around to accomplish something good, and although I was never 'officially' born, I lived. God used me in his great wisdom and mercy, to save many lives.

I know if my mother had truly known me, she would not have done what she did; and I know there will be many who read my story that have already made the same regrettable decision my mother made. Don't be discouraged or lose heart; just do what my mother did: run to the same precious loving arms that brought her forgiveness, comfort and peace.

My voice has been silenced, but yours can still be heard. I beg of you, for the sake of my sisters and brothers, who are right now enduring my fate, do not be silent. Every conceived child is a living soul, and it is my earnest plea that you accept this fact; so you, along with many others, can save even more lives.

Consider this: A pre-born baby's heart beats about 40 million times before birth. They hear their mother's voice, and those voices around her. They feel pain and at times feel uncomfortable in their small, confined space. At times they are content, at times fearful. They are persons, if not to the world, to God, living souls with their own unique DNA, blood type and one-of-a-kind fingerprints; and they have a name: mine *is* Jeni Ann Johnson.

The law, a stroke of the pen, allowed my life, and millions of others like me to be barbarically murdered and thrown into a garbage can, like common trash.

Those of you who are currently pregnant, please don't think that one day you will *become* a mother, but realize in fact, that you already *are* a mother; with a precious soul, an independent life already living in you! My mother dreamt a life that she will never have with me. But it isn't too late for you. You have both the privilege and opportunity to live out a real-life story with your precious child.

With earnest sincerity,
Jeni

"Before I formed you in the womb, I knew you. . ."

JEREMIAH 1:5

Let Me Live

If I took another's breath away,
If I took their food, so they would waste away,
And if I made their heart cease to beat,
Or with a knife, made their flesh to bleed,
What would a jury's verdict be?
What would that victim say to me?

Let me live, let me live, let me live to see another day,
Let me live to see my mother's face I pray, let me live

A million martyrs this year may fall,
Each death justified by freedom's call.
And each drop of blood cries to the throne of God,
While the judgment of each one falls on us all.
Now what would that jury's verdict be?
Their innocence cry out to you and me

Let me live, let me live, let me live to see another day,
Let me live to see my mother's face I pray, let me live

And their silent screams, though not heard by man,
Are heard by the heavenly angel band as they sing

Oh come angel band, Come and around me stand,
Carry me away on your snow-white wings to my eternal home,
Carry me away on your snow-white wings to my eternal home.

Looking Back

My mother told me the other day,
Just before the Lord took her away.
Son I never told you before,
But, you were almost never born.

I was young and all alone,
And had to choose between right and wrong.
Give you up to hide my shame,
Or give you life and bare the pain.

Looking back, I see all the faces,
Of friends and places that I would have missed.
Looking back, though sometimes through pain,
I would not have known love like this,
Looking back, looking back, I have no regrets,
Looking back.

Looking down upon her face,
I see the peace of God's grace.
And I'm glad she choose to let me live,
'Cause of all the love that we shared through it.

Looking back, I see all the faces,
Of friends and places that I would have missed.
Looking back, though sometimes through pain,
I would not have known love like this,
Looking back, looking back, I have no regrets,
Looking back.

A Mother's Lament

(Warning: Spoiler alert in these lyrics)

Jeni as a young girl wasn't always an angel.
But, oh how much I loved her through it all.
And, no matter how hard the hard times,
we were always there for each other.
I'm so glad she came into my life.

Jeni stands today, Michael by her side,
Hand in hand to say their wedding vows.
But, something doesn't seem right,
I feel it deep inside,
As I awake to see a doctor's face, I realize.

Jeni won't marry Michael in this lifetime,
'Cause, Jeni won't be around to say, "I do."
Jeni won't marry Michael in this lifetime.
'Cause I made that choice for her,
But I thought that I was making it for me.

Now, I was told just another choice,
To be made in the name of freedom.
So, why do I feel so lonely in my soul?
Could it be I was mistaken, as I walk out of this door;
'Cause I'll never see my Jeni anymore.

Jeni won't marry Michael in this lifetime,
'Cause, Jeni won't be around to say, "I do."
Jeni won't marry Michael in this lifetime.
'Cause I made that choice for her,
But I thought that I was making it for me.

COPYRIGHT 1994—eternalsoulministries.com
"Praise God from whom all blessing flow."

Biography

LEE GANDER was called to the ministry at an early age, and has dedicated his life to preaching the Good News, setting the captive free, and championing the innocent, those silent voices that cannot speak for themselves. A prolific writer of over 400 songs and an accomplished musician, Lee is now venturing in this new direction as author, with a desire to passionately broaden the message of God's redemptive love for the lost and hurting around him.